ASSIGNMENT IN ETERNITY

Volume II

ASSIGNMENT IN ETERNITY
Volume II

Robert A. Heinlein

NEW ENGLISH LIBRARY/TIMES MIRROR

For Sprague and Catherine

First NEL paperback edition September 1978

NEL Books are published by
New English Library Limited from
Barnard's Inn, Holborn,
London EC1N 2JR
Made and printed in Great Britain by
Hazell Watson & Viney Ltd,
Aylesbury, Bucks

45003759 2

LOST LEGACY

CHAPTER ONE

"YE HAVE EYES TO SEE WITH!"

"HI-YAH, BUTCHER!" Doctor Philip Huxley put down the dice cup he had been fiddling with as he spoke, and shoved out a chair with his foot. "Sit down."

The man addressed ostentatiously ignored the salutation while handing a yellow slicker and soggy felt hat to the Faculty Clubroom attendant, but accepted the chair. His first words were to the negro attendant.

"Did you hear that, Pete? A witch doctor, passing himself off as a psychologist, has the effrontery to refer to me—to *me*, a licensed physician and surgeon, as a butcher." His voice was filled with gentle reproach.

"Don't let him kid you, Pete. If Doctor Coburn ever got you into an operating theatre, he'd open up your head just to see what makes you tick. He'd use your skull to make an ashtray."

The colored man grinned as he wiped the table, but said nothing.

Coburn clucked and shook his head. "That from a witch doctor. Still looking for the Little Man Who Wasn't There, Phil?"

"If you mean parapsychology, yes."

"How's the racket coming?"

"Pretty good. I've got one less lecture this semester, which is just as well—I get awfully tired of explaining to the wide-eyed innocents how little we really know about what goes on inside their think-tanks. I'd rather do research."

"Who wouldn't? Struck any pay dirt lately?"

"Some. I'm having a lot of fun with a law student just now, chap named Valdez."

Coburn lifted his brows. "So? E.S.P.?"

"Kinda. He's sort of a clairvoyant; if he can see one side of an object, he can see the other side, too."

"Nuts!"

" 'If you're so smart, why ain't you rich?' I've tried him out under carefully controlled conditions, and he can do it—see around corners."

"Hmmmm—well, as my Grandfather Stonebender used to say, 'God has more aces up his sleeve than were ever dealt in the game.' He would be a menace at stud poker."

"Matter of fact, he made his stake for law school as a professional gambler."

"Found out how he does it?"

"No, damn it." Huxley drummed on the table top, a worried look on his face. "If I just had a little money for research, I might get enough data to make this sort of thing significant. Look at what Rhine accomplished at Duke."

"Well, why don't you holler? Go before the Board and bite 'em in the ear for it. Tell 'em how you're going to make Western University famous."

Huxley looked still more morose. "Fat chance. I talked with my dean and he wouldn't even let me take it up with the President. Scared that the old fathead will clamp down on the department even more than he has. You see, officially, we are supposed to be behaviorists. Any suggestion that there might be something to consciousness that can't be explained in terms of physiology and mechanics is about as welcome as a Saint Bernard in a telephone booth."

The telephone signal glowed red back of the attendant's counter. He switched off the newscast and answered the call. "Hello . . . Yes, ma'am, he is. I'll call him. Telephone for you, Doctuh Coburn."

"Switch it over here." Coburn turned the telephone panel at the table around so that it faced him; as he did so it lighted up with the face of a young woman. He picked up the handset. "What is it? . . . What's that? How long ago did it happen? . . . Who made the diagnosis? . . . Read that over again . . . Let me see the chart." He inspected its image reflected in

8

the panel, then added, "Very well. I'll be right over. Prepare the patient for operating." He switched off the instrument and turned to Huxley. "Got to go, Phil—emergency."

"What sort?"

"It'll interest you. Trephining. Maybe some cerebral excision. Car accident. Come along and watch it, if you have time." He was putting on his slicker as he spoke. He turned and swung out the west door with a long, loose-limbed stride. Huxley grabbed his own raincoat and hurried to catch up with him.

"How come," he asked as he came abreast, "they had to search for you?"

"Left my pocketphone in my other suit," Coburn returned briefly. "On purpose—I wanted a little peace and quiet. No luck."

They worked north and west through the arcades and passages that connected the Union with the Science group, ignoring the moving walkways as being too slow. But when they came to the conveyor subway under Third Avenue opposite the Pottenger Medical School, they found it flooded, its machinery stalled, and were forced to detour west to the Fairfax Avenue conveyor. Coburn cursed impartially the engineers and the planning commission for the fact that spring brings torrential rains to Southern California, Chamber of Commerce or no.

They got rid of their wet clothes in the Physicians' Room and moved on to the gowning room for surgery. An orderly helped Huxley into white trousers and cotton shoe covers, and they moved to the next room to scrub. Coburn invited Huxley to scrub also in order that he might watch the operation close up. For three minutes by the little sand glass they scrubbed away with strong green soap, then stepped through a door and were gowned and gloved by silent, efficient nurses. Huxley felt rather silly to be helped on with his clothes by a nurse who had to stand on tip-toe to get the sleeves high enough. They were ushered through the glass door into surgery III, rubber-covered hands held out, as if holding a skein of yarn.

The patient was already in place on the table, head raised up and skull clamped immobile. Someone snapped a switch and a merciless circle of blue-white lights beat down on the only portion of him that was exposed, the right side of his skull. Coburn glanced quickly around the room, Huxley following his glance—light green walls, two operating nurses, gowned, masked, and hooded into sexlessness, a 'dirty' nurse, busy with something in the corner, the anesthetist, the instruments that told Coburn the state of the patient's heart action and respiration.

A nurse held the chart for the surgeon to read. At a word from Coburn, the anesthetist uncovered the patient's face for a moment. Lean brown face, aquiline nose, closed sunken eyes. Huxley repressed an exclamation. Coburn raised his eyebrows at Huxley.

"What's the trouble?"

"It's Juan Valdez!"

"Who's he?"

"The one I was telling you about—the law student with the trick eyes."

"Hmm—Well, his trick eyes didn't see around enough corners this time. He's lucky to be alive. You'll see better, Phil, if you stand over there."

Coburn changed to impersonal efficiency, ignored Huxley's presence and concentrated the whole of his able intellect on the damaged flesh before him. The skull had been crushed, or punched, apparently by coming into violent contact with some hard object with moderately sharp edges. The wound lay above the right ear, and was, superficially, two inches, or more, across. It was impossible, before exploration, to tell just how much damage had been suffered by the bony structure and the grey matter behind.

Undoubtedly there was some damage to the brain itself. The wound had been cleaned up on the surface and the area around it shaved and painted. The trauma showed up as a definite hole in the cranium. It was bleeding slightly and was partly filled with a curiously nauseating conglomerate of clotted purple blood, white tissue, grey tissue, pale yellow tissue.

The surgeon's lean slender fingers, unhuman in their pale orange coverings, moved gently, deftly in the wound, as if imbued with a separate life and intelligence of their own. Destroyed tissue, too freshly dead for the component cells to realize it, was cleared away,—chipped fragments of bone, lacerated mater dura, the grey cortical tissue of the cerebrum itself.

Huxley became fascinated by the minuscule drama, lost track of time, and of the sequence of events. He remembered terse orders for assistance. "Clamp!" "Retractor!" "Sponge!" The sound of the tiny saw, a muffled whine, then the tooth-tingling grind it made in cutting through solid living bone. Gently a spatulate instrument was used to straighten out the tortured convolutions. Incredible and unreal, he watched a scalpel whittle at the door of the mind, shave the thin wall of reason.

Three times a nurse wiped sweat from the surgeon's face.

Wax performed its function. Vitallium alloy replaced bone, dressing shut out infection. Huxley had watched uncounted operations, but felt again that almost insupportable sense of relief and triumph that comes when the surgeon turns away, and begins stripping off his gloves as he heads for the gowning room.

When Huxley joined Coburn, the surgeon had doused his mask and cap, and was feeling under his gown for cigarets. He looked entirely human again. He grinned at Huxley and inquired,

"Well, how did you like it?"

"Swell. It was the first time I was able to watch that type of thing so closely. You can't see so well from behind the glass, you know. Is he going to be all right?"

Coburn's expression changed. "He is a friend of yours, isn't he? That had slipped my mind for the moment. Sorry.

He'll be all right, I'm pretty sure. He's young and strong, and he came through the operation very nicely. You can come see for yourself in a couple of days."

"You excised quite a lot of the speech center, didn't you? Will he be able to talk when he gets well? Isn't he likely to have aphasia, or some other speech disorder?"

"Speech center? Why, I wasn't even close to the speech centers."

"Huh?"

"Put a rock in your right hand, Phil, so you'll know it next time. You're turned around a hundred and eighty degrees. I was working in the *right* cerebral lobe, not the left lobe."

Huxley looked puzzled, spread both hands out in front of him, glanced from one to the other, then his face cleared and he laughed. "You're right. You know, I have the damndest time with that. I never can remember which way to deal in a bridge game. But wait a minute—I had it so firmly fixed in my mind that you were on the left side in the speech centers that I am confused. What do you think the result will be on his neurophysiology?"

"Nothing—if past experience is any criterion. What I took away he'll never miss. I was working in terra incognito, pal— No Man's Land. If that portion of the brain that I was in has any function, the best physiologists haven't been able to prove it."

CHAPTER TWO

THREE BLIND MICE

BRRRINNG!

Joan Freeman reached out blindly with one hand and shut off the alarm clock, her eyes jammed shut in the vain belief that she could remain asleep if she did. Her mind wondered. Sunday. Don't have to get up early on Sunday. Then why had she set the alarm? She remembered suddenly and rolled out of bed, warm feet on a floor cold in the morning air. Her pajamas landed on that floor as she landed in the shower, yelled, turned the shower to warm, then back to cold again.

The last item from the refrigerator had gone into a basket, and a thermos jug was filled by the time she heard the sound of a car on the hill outside, the crunch of tires on granite in the driveway. She hurriedly pulled on short boots, snapped the loops of her jodhpurs under them, and looked at herself in the mirror. Not bad, she thought. Not Miss America, but she wouldn't frighten any children.

A banging at the door was echoed by the doorbell, and a baritone voice, "Joan! Are you decent?"

"Practically. Come on in, Phil."

Huxley, in slacks and polo shirt, was followed by another figure. He turned to him. "Joan, this is Ben Coburn, Doctor Ben Coburn. Doctor Coburn, Miss Freeman."

"Awfully nice of you to let me come, Miss Freeman."

"Not at all, Doctor. Phil had told me so much about you that I have been anxious to meet you." The conventionalities flowed with the ease of all long-established tribal taboo.

"Call him Ben, Joan. It's good for his ego."

While Joan and Phil loaded the car Coburn looked over the young woman's studio house. A single large room, panelled in knotty pine and dominated by a friendly fieldstone fireplace set about with untidy bookcases, gave evidence of her personality. He had stepped through open french doors into a tiny patio, paved with mossy bricks and fitted with a barbecue pit and a little fishpond, brilliant in the morning sunlight, when he heard himself called.

"Doc! Stir your stumps! Time's awastin'!"

He glanced again around the patio, and rejoined the others at the car. "I like your house, Miss Freeman. Why should we bother to leave Beachwood Drive when Griffith Park can't be any pleasanter?"

"That's easy. If you stay at home, it's not a picnic—it's just breakfast. My name's Joan."

"May I put in a request for 'just breakfast' here some morning—Joan?"

"Lay off o' that mug, Joan," advised Phil in a stage whisper. "His intentions ain't honorable."

Joan straightened up the remains of what had recently been a proper-sized meal. She chucked into the fire three well-picked bones to which thick sirloin steaks were no longer attached, added some discarded wrapping paper and one lonely roll. She shook the thermos jug. It gurgled slightly. "Anybody want some more grapefruit juice?" she called.

"Any more coffee?" asked Coburn, then continued to Huxley, "His special talents are gone completely?"

"Plenty," Joan replied. "Serve yourselves."

The Doctor filled his own cup and Huxley's. Phil answered, "Gone entirely, I'm reasonably certain. I thought it might be hysterical shock from the operation, but I tried him under hypnosis, and the results were still negative—completely. Joan, you're some cook. Will you adopt me?"

"You're over twenty-one."

"I could easily have him certified as incompetent," volunteered Coburn.

"Single women aren't favored for adoption."

"Marry me, and it will be all right—we can both adopt him and you can cook for all of us."

"Well, I won't say that I won't and I won't say that I will, but I will say that it's the best offer I've had today. What were you guys talking about?"

"Make him put it in writing, Joan. We were talking about Valdez."

"Oh! You were going to run those last tests yesterday, weren't you? How did you come out?"

"Absolutely negative insofar as his special clairvoyance was concerned. It's gone."

"Hmm—How about the control tests?"

"The Humm-Wadsworth Temperament Test showed exactly the same profile as before the accident, within the inherent limits of accuracy of the technique. His intelligence quotient came within the technique limit, too. Association tests didn't show anything either. By all the accepted standards of neuropsychology he is the same individual, except in two respects; he's minus a chunk of his cortex, and he is no longer able to see around corners. Oh, yes, and he's annoyed at losing that ability."

After a pause she answered, "That's pretty conclusive, isn't it?"

Huxley turned to Coburn. "What do you think, Ben?"

"Well, I don't know. You are trying to get me to admit that that piece of grey matter I cut out of his head gave him the ability to see in a fashion not possible to normal sense organs and not accounted for by orthodox medical theory, aren't you?"

"I'm not trying to make you admit anything. I'm trying to find out something."

"Well, since you put it that way, I would say if we stipulate that all your primary data were obtained with care under properly controlled conditions—"

"They were."

"—and that you have exercised even greater care in obtaining your negative secondary data—"

"I have. Damn it, I tried for three weeks under all conceivable conditions."

"Then we have the inescapable conclusions, first—" He ticked them off on his fingers. "—that this subject could see without the intervention of physical sense organs; and second, that this unusual, to put it mildly, ability was in some way related to a portion of his cerebrum in the dexter lobe."

"Bravo!" This was Joan's contribution.

"Thanks, Ben," acknowledged Phil. "I had reached the same conclusions, of course, but it's very encouraging to have someone else agree with me."

"Well, now that you are there, where are you?"

"I don't know exactly. Let me put it this way; I got into psychology for the same reason a person joins a church—because he feels an overpowering need to understand himself and the world around him. When I was a young student, I thought modern psychology could tell me the answers, but I soon found out that the best psychologists didn't know a damn thing about the real core of the matter. Oh, I am not disparaging the work that has been done; it was badly needed and has been very useful in its way. None of 'em know what life is, what thought is, whether free will is a reality or an illusion, or whether that last question means anything. The best of 'em admit their ignorance; the worst of them make dogmatic assertions that are obvious absurdities—for example some of the mechanistic behaviorists that think just because Pavlov could condition a dog to drool at the sound of a bell that, therefore, they knew all about how Paderewski made music!"

Joan, who had been lying quietly in the shade of the big liveoaks and listening, spoke up. "Ben, you are a brain surgeon, aren't you?"

"One of the best," certified Phil.

"You've seen a lot of brains, furthermore you've seen 'em while they were *alive*, which is more than most psychologists have. What do you believe thought is? What do you think makes us tick?"

He grinned at her. "You've got me, kid. I don't pretend to know. It's not my business; I'm just a tinker."

She sat up. "Give me a cigaret, Phil. I've arrived just where Phil is, but by a different road. My father wanted me to study law. I soon found out that I was more interested in the principles behind law and I changed over to the School of Philosophy. But philosophy wasn't the answer. There really isn't anything to philosophy. Did you ever eat that cotton candy they sell at fairs? Well, philosophy is like that—it looks as if it were really something, and it's awfully pretty, and it tastes sweet, but when you go to bite it you can't get your teeth into it, and when you try to swallow, there isn't anything there. Philosophy is word-chasing, as significant as a puppy chasing its tail.

"I was about to get my Ph.D. in the School of Philosophy, when I chucked it and came to the science division and started taking courses in psychology. I thought that if I was a good little girl and patient, all would be revealed to me. Well, Phil has told us what that leads to. I began to think about studying medicine, or biology. You just gave the show away on that. Maybe it was a mistake to teach women to read and write."

Ben laughed. "This seems to be experience meeting at the village church; I might as well make my confession. I guess most medical men start out with a desire to know all about man and what makes him tick, but it's a big field, the final answers are elusive and there is always so much work that needs to be done right now, that we quit worrying about the final problems. I'm as interested as I ever was in knowing what life, and thought, and so forth, really are, but I have to have an attack of insomnia to find time to worry about them. Phil, are you seriously proposing to tackle such things?"

"In a way, yes. I've been gathering data on all sorts of phenomena that run contrary to orthodox psychological theory—all the junk that goes under the general name of metapsychics—telepathy, clairvoyance, so-called psychic manifestations, clairaudience, levitation, yoga stuff, stigmata, anything of that sort I can find."

"Don't you find that most of that stuff can be explained in an ordinary fashion?"

"Quite a lot of it, sure. Then you can strain orthodox theory all out of shape and ignore the statistical laws of probability to account for most of the rest. Then by attributing anything that is left over to charlatanism, credulity, and self-hypnosis, and refuse to investigate it, you can go peacefully back to sleep."

"Occam's razor," murmured Joan.

"Huh?"

"William of Occam's Razor. It's a name for a principle in logic; whenever two hypotheses both cover the facts, use the simpler of the two. When a conventional scientist has to strain his orthodox theories all out of shape, 'til they resemble something thought up by Rube Goldberg, to account for unorthodox phenomena, he's ignoring the principle of Occam's Razor. It's simpler to draw up a new hypothesis to cover all the facts than to strain an old one that was never intended to cover the non-conforming data. But scientists are more attached to their theories than they are to their wives and families."

"My," said Phil admiringly, "to think that that came out from under a permanent wave."

"If you'll hold him, Ben, I'll beat him with this here thermos jug."

"I apologize. You're absolutely right, darling. I decided to forget about theories, to treat these outcast phenomena like any ordinary data, and to see where it landed me."

"What sort of stuff," put in Ben, "have you dug up, Phil?"

"Quite a variety, some verified, some mere rumor, a little of it carefully checked under laboratory conditions, like Valdez. Of course, you've heard of all the stunts attributed to Yoga. Very little of it has been duplicated in the Western Hemisphere, which counts against it; nevertheless a lot of odd stuff in India has been reported by competent, cool-minded observers—telepathy, accurate soothsaying, clairvoyance, fire walking, and so forth."

"Why do you include fire walking in metapsychics?"

"On the chance that the mind can control the body and other material objects in some esoteric fashion."

"Hmm."

"Is the idea any more marvelous than the fact that you can cause your hand to scratch your head? We haven't any more idea of the actual workings of volition on matter in one case than in the other. Take the Tierra del Fuegans. They slept on the ground, naked, even in zero weather. Now the body can't make any such adjustment in its economy. It hasn't the machinery; any physiologist will tell you so. A naked human being caught outdoors in zero weather must exercise, or die. But the Tierra del Fuegans didn't know about metabolic rates and such. They just slept—nice, and warm, and cozy."

"So far you haven't mentioned anything close to home. If you are going to allow that much latitude, my Grandfather Stonebender had much more wonderful experiences."

"I'm coming to them. Don't forget Valdez."

"What's this about Ben's grandfather?" asked Joan.

"Joan, don't ever boast about anything in Ben's presence. You'll find that his Grandfather Stonebender did it faster, easier, and better."

A look of more-in-sorrow-than-in-anger shone out of Coburn's pale blue eyes. "Why, Phil, I'm surprised at you. If I weren't a Stonebender myself, and tolerant, I'd be inclined to resent that remark. But your apology is accepted."

"Well, to bring matters closer home, besides Valdez, there was a man in my home town, Springfield, Missouri, who had a clock in his head."

"What do you mean?"

"I mean he knew the exact time without looking at a clock. If your watch disagreed with him, your watch was wrong. Besides that, he was a lightning calculator—knew the answer instantly to the most complicated problems in arithmetic you cared to put to him. In other ways he was feeble-minded."

Ben nodded. "It's a common phenomenon—*idiots savants.*"

"But giving it a name doesn't explain it. Besides which, while a number of the people with erratic talents are feeble-minded, not all of them are. I believe that by far the greater per cent of them are not, but that we rarely hear of them because the intelligent ones are smart enough to know that they would be annoyed by the crowd, possibly persecuted, if they let the rest of us suspect that they were different."

Ben nodded again. "You got something there, Phil. Go ahead."

"There have been a lot of these people with impossible talents who were not subnormal in other ways and who were right close to home. Boris Sidis, for example—"

"He was that child prodigy, wasn't he? I thought he played out?"

"Maybe. Personally, I think he grew cagy and decided not to let the other monkeys know that he was different. In any case he had a lot of remarkable talents, in intensity, if not in kind. He must have been able to read a page of print just by glancing at it, and he undoubtedly had complete memory. Speaking of complete memory, how about Blind Tom, the negro pianist who could play any piece of music he had ever heard once? Nearer home, there was this boy right here in Los Angeles County not so very many years ago who could play ping-pong blind-folded, or anything else, for which normal people require eyes. I checked him myself, and he could do it. And there was the 'Instantaneous Echo.'"

"You never told me about him, Phil," commented Joan. "What could he do?"

"He could talk along with you, using your words and intonations, in any language whether he knew the language or not. And he would keep pace with you so accurately that anyone listening wouldn't be able to tell the two of you apart. He could imitate your speech and words as immediately, as accurately, and as effortlessly as your shadow follows the movements of your body."

"Pretty fancy, what? And rather difficult to explain by

20

behaviorist theory. Ever run across any cases of levitation, Phil?"

"Not of human beings. However I have seen a local medium—a nice kid, non-professional, used to live next door to me—make articles of furniture in my own house rise up off the floor and float. I was cold sober. It either happened or I was hypnotized; have it your own way. Speaking of levitating, you know the story they tell about Nijinsky?"

"Which one?"

"About him floating. There are thousands of people here and in Europe (unless they died in the Collapse) who testify that in *Le Spectre de la Rose* he used to leap up into the air, pause for a while, then come down when he got ready. Call it mass hallucination—I didn't see it."

"Occam's Razor again," said Joan.

"So?"

"Mass hallucination is harder to explain than one man's floating in the air for a few seconds. Mass hallucination not proved—mustn't infer it to get rid of a troublesome fact. It's comparable to the 'There aint no sech animal' of the yokel who saw the rhinoceros for the first time."

"Maybe so. Any other sort of trick stuff you want to hear about, Ben? I got a million of 'em."

"How about forerunners, and telepathy?"

"Well, telepathy is positively proved, though still unexplained, by Dr Rhine's experiments. Of course a lot of people had observed it before then, with such frequency as to make questioning it unreasonable. Mark Twain, for example. He wrote about it fifty years before Rhine, with documentation and circumstantial detail. He wasn't a scientist, but he had hard common sense and shouldn't have been ignored. Upton Sinclair, too. Forerunners are a little harder. Everyone has heard dozens of stories of hunches that came true, but they are hard to follow up in most cases. You might try J. W. Dunne's *Experiment with Time* for a scientific record under controlled conditions of forerunners in dreams."

"Where does all this get you, Phil? You aren't just collecting Believe-it-or-nots?"

"No, but I had to assemble a pile of data—you ought to look over my notebooks—before I could formulate a working hypothesis. I have one now."

"Well?"

"You gave it to me—by operating on Valdez. I had begun to suspect sometime ago that these people with odd and apparently impossible mental and physical abilities were no different from the rest of us in any sense of abnormality, but that they had stumbled on potentialities inherent in all of us. Tell me, when you had Valdez' cranium open did you notice anything abnormal in its appearance?"

"No. Aside from the wound, it presented no special features."

"Very well. Yet when you excised that damaged portion, he no longer possessed his strange clairvoyant power. You took that chunk of his brain out of an uncharted area—no known function. Now it is a primary datum of psychology and physiology that large areas of the brain have no *known* function. It doesn't seem reasonable that the most highly developed and highly specialized part of the body should have large areas with *no* function; it is more reasonable to assume that the functions are unknown. And yet men have had large pieces of their cortices cut out without any *apparent* loss in their mental powers—as long as the areas controlling the normal functions of the body were left untouched.

"Now in this one case, Valdez, we have established a direct connection between an uncharted area of the brain and an odd talent, to wit, clairvoyance. My working hypothesis comes directly from that: All normal people are potentially able to exercise all (or possibly most) of the odd talents we have referred to—telepathy, clairvoyance, special mathematical ability, special control over the body and its functions, and so forth. The potential ability to do these things is lodged in the unassigned areas of the brain."

Coburn pursed his lips. "Mmm—I don't know. If we all

have these wonderful abilities, which isn't proved, how is it that we don't seem able to use them?"

"I haven't proved anything—yet. This is a working hypothesis. But let me give you an analogy. These abilities aren't like sight, hearing, and touch which we can't avoid using from birth; they are more like the ability to talk, which has its own special centers in the brain from birth, *but which has to be trained into being*. Do you think a child raised exclusively by deaf-mutes would ever learn to talk? Of course not. To outward appearance he would be a deaf-mute."

"I give up," conceded Coburn. "You set up an hypothesis and made it plausible. But how are you going to check it? I don't see any place to get hold of it. It's a very pretty speculation, but without a working procedure, it's just fantasy."

Huxley rolled over and stared unhappily up through the branches. 'That's the rub. I've lost my best wild talent case. I don't know where to begin."

"But, Phil," protested Joan. "You want normal subjects, and then try to develop special abilities in them. I think it's wonderful. When do we start?"

"When do we start what?"

"On *me*, of course. Take that ability to do lightning calculations, for example. If you could develop that in me, you'd be a magician. I got bogged down in first year algebra. I don't know the multiplication tables even now!"

CHAPTER THREE

"EVERY MAN HIS OWN GENIUS"

"SHALL WE GET BUSY?" asked Phil.

"Oh, let's not," Joan objected. "Let's drink our coffee in peace and let dinner settle. We haven't seen Ben for two weeks. I want to hear what he's been doing up in San Francisco."

"Thanks, darling," the doctor answered, "but I'd much rather hear about the Mad Scientist and his Trilby."

"Trilby, hell," Huxley protested, "She's as independent as a hog on ice. However, we've got something to show you this time, Doc."

"Really? That's good. What?"

"Well, as you know, we didn't make much progress for the first couple of months. It was all up hill. Joan developed a fair telepathic ability, but it was erratic and unreliable. As for mathematical ability, she had learned her multiplication tables, but as for being a lightning calculator, she was a washout."

Joan jumped up, crossed between the men and the fireplace, and entered her tiny Pullman kitchen. "I've got to scrape these dishes and put them to soak before the ants get at 'em. Talk loud, so I can hear you."

"What can Joan do now, Phil?"

"I'm not going to tell you. You wait and see. Joan! Where's the card table?"

"Back of the couch. No need to shout. I can hear plainly since I got my Foxy Grandma Stream-lined Ear Trumpet."

"Okay, wench, I found it. Cards in the usual place?"

"Yes, I'll be with you in a moment." She reappeared, whisking off a giddy kitchen apron, and sat down on the couch, hugging her knees. 'The Great Gaga, the Ghoul of

24

Hollywood is ready. Sees all, knows all, and tells a darnsight more. Fortunetelling, teethpulling, and refined entertainment for the entire family."

"Cut out the clowning. We'll start out with a little straight telepathy. Throw every thing else out of gear. Shuffle the cards, Ben."

Coburn did so. "Now what?"

"Deal 'em off, one at a time, letting you and me see 'em, but not Joan. Call 'em off, kid."

Ben dealt them out slowly. Joan commenced to recite in a sing-song voice, "Seven of diamonds; jack of hearts; ace of hearts; three of spades; ten of diamonds; six of clubs; nine of spades; eight of clubs—"

"Ben, that's the first time I've ever seen you look amazed."

"Right through the deck without a mistake. Grandfather Stonebender couldn't have done better."

"That's high praise, chum. Let's try a variation. I'll sit out this one. Don't let me see them. I don't know how it will work, as we never worked with anyone else. Try it."

A few minutes later Coburn put down the last card. "Perfect! Not a mistake."

Joan got up and came over to the table. "How come this deck has two tens of hearts in it?" She riffled through the deck, and pulled out one card. "Oh! You thought the seventh card was the ten of hearts; it was the ten of diamonds. See?"

"I guess I did," Ben admitted. "I'm sorry I threw you a curve. The light isn't any too good."

"Joan prefers artistic lighting effects to saving her eyes," explained Phil. "I'm glad it happened; it shows she was using telepathy, not clairvoyance. Now for a spot of mathematics. We'll skip the usual stunts like cube roots, instantaneous addition, logarithms of hyperbolic functions, and stuff. Take my word for it; she can do 'em. You can try her later on those simple tricks. Here's a little honey I shot in my own kitchen. It involves fast reading, complete memory, handling of unbelievable number of permutations and combinations, and mathematical investigation of alternatives. You play solitaire, Ben?"

"Sure."

"I want you to shuffle the cards thoroughly, then lay out a Canfield solitaire, dealing from left to right, then play it out, three cards at a time, going through the deck again and again, until you are stuck and can't go any farther."

"Okay. What's the gag?"

"After you have shuffled and cut, I want you to riffle the cards through once, holding them up so that Joan gets a quick glimpse of the index on each card. Then wait a moment."

Silently he did what he had been asked to do. Joan checked him. "You'll have to do it again, Ben. I saw only fifty-one cards."

"Two of them must have stuck together. I'll do it more carefully." He repeated it.

"Fifty-two that time. That's fine."

"Are you ready, Joan?"

"Yes, Phil. Take it down; hearts to the six, diamonds to the four, spades to the deuce, no clubs."

Coburn looked incredulous. "Do you mean that is the way this game is going to come out?"

"Try it and see."

He dealt the cards out from left to right, then played the game out slowly. Joan stopped him at one point. "No, play the king of hearts' stack into that space, rather than the king of spades. The king of spades play would have gotten the ace of clubs out, but three less hearts would play out if you did so." Coburn made no comment, but did as she told him to do. Twice more she stopped him and indicated a different choice of alternatives.

The game played out exactly as she had predicted.

Coburn ran his hand through his hair and stared at the cards. "Joan," he said meekly, "does your head ever ache?"

"Not from doing that stuff. It doesn't seem to be an effort at all."

"You know," put in Phil, seriously, "there isn't any real reason why it should be a strain. So far as we know, thinking requires no expenditure of energy at all. A person ought to be able to think straight and accurately with no effort. I've a notion that it is faulty thinking that makes headaches."

"But how in the devil does she do it, Phil? It makes my head ache just to try to imagine the size of that problem, if it were worked out long hand by conventional mathematics."

"I don't know how she does it. Neither does she."

"Then how did she *learn* to do it?"

"We'll take that up later. First, I want to show you our *piece de resistance*."

"I can't take much more. I'm groggy now."

"You'll like this."

"Wait a minute, Phil. I want to try one of my own. How fast can Joan read?"

"As fast as she can see."

"Hmm—". The doctor hauled a sheaf of typewritten pages out of his inside pocket. "I've got the second draft of a paper I've been working on. Let's try Joan on a page of it. Okay, Joan?"

He separated an inner page from the rest and handed it to her. She glanced at it and handed it back at once. He looked puzzled and said:

"What's the matter?"

"Nothing. Check me as I read back." She started in a rapid singsong, " 'page four. —now according to Cunningham, fifth edition, page 547,: "Another strand of fibres, videlicet, the fasciculus spinocerebellaris (posterior), prolonged upwards in the lateral furniculus of the medulla spinallis, gradually leaves this portion of the medulla oblongata. This tract lies on the surface, and is—"

"That's enough, Joan, hold it. God knows how you did it, but you read and memorized that page of technical junk in a split second." He grinned slyly. "But your pronunciation

27

was a bit spotty. Grandfather Stonebender's would have been perfect."

"What can you expect? I don't know what half of the words mean."

"Joan, how did you learn to do all this stuff?"

"Truthfully, Doctor, I don't know. It's something like learning to ride a bicycle—you take one spill after another, then one day you get on and just ride away, easy as you please. And in a week you are riding without handle-bars and trying stunts. It's been like that—I knew what I wanted to do, and one day I could. Come on, Phil's getting impatient."

Ben maintained a puzzled silence and permitted Phil to lead him to a little desk in the corner. "Joan, can we use any drawer? OK. Ben, pick out a drawer in this desk, remove any articles you wish, add anything you wish. Then, without looking into the drawer, stir up the contents and remove a few articles and drop them into another drawer. I want to eliminate the possibility of telepathy."

"Phil, don't worry about my housekeeping. My large staff of secretaries will be only too happy to straighten out that desk after you get through playing with it."

"Don't stand in the way of science, little one. Besides," he added, glancing into a drawer, "this desk obviously hasn't been straightened for at least six months. A little more stirring up won't hurt it."

"Humph! What can you expect when I spend all my time learning parlor tricks for you? Besides, I know where everything is."

"That's just what I am afraid of, and why I want Ben to introduce a little more of the random element—if possible. Go ahead, Ben."

When the doctor had complied and closed the drawer, Phil continued, "Better use pencil and paper on this one, Joan. First list everything you see in the drawer, then draw a little sketch to show approximate locations and arrangement."

"OK." She sat down at the desk and commenced to write rapidly:

One large black leather handbag

Six-inch ruler

Ben stopped her. "Wait a minute. This is all wrong. I would have noticed anything as big as a handbag."

She wrinkled her brow. "Which drawer did you say?"

"The second on the right."

"I thought you said the top drawer."

"Well, perhaps I did."

She started again:

Brass paper knife

Six assorted pencils and a red pencil

Thirteen rubber bands

Pearl-handled penknife

"That must be your knife, Ben. It's very pretty; why haven't I seen it before?"

"I bought it in San Francisco. Good God, girl. You haven't seen it *yet*."

One paper of matches, advertising the Sir Francis Drake Hotel

Eight letters and two bills

Two ticket stubs, the Follies Burlesque Theatre—"Doctor, I'm *surprised* at you."

"Get on with your knitting."

"Provided you promise to take me the next time you go."

One fever thermometer with a pocket clip

Art gum and a typewriter eraser

Three keys, assorted

One lipstick, Max Factor #3

A scratch pad and some file cards, used on one side

One small brown paper sack containing one pair stockings, size nine, shade Creole. —"I'd forgotten that I had bought them; I searched all through the house for a decent pair this morning."

"Why didn't you just use your X-ray eyes, Mrs. Houdini?"

She looked startled. "Do you know, it just didn't occur to me. I haven't gotten around to trying to *use* this stuff yet."

"Anything else in the drawer?"

"Nothing but a box of notepaper. Just a sec: I'll make the sketch." She sketched busily for a couple of minutes, her tongue between her teeth, her eyes darting from the paper toward the closed drawer and back again. Ben inquired,

"Do you have to look in the direction of the drawer to see inside it?"

"No, but it helps. It makes me dizzy to *see* a thing when I am looking away from it."

The contents and arrangement of the drawer were checked and found to be exactly as Joan had stated they were. Doctor Coburn sat quietly, making no comment, when they had finished. Phil, slightly irked at his lack of demonstrativeness, spoke to him.

"Well, Ben, what did you think of it? How did you like it?"

"You know what I thought of it. You've proved your theory up to the hilt—but I'm thinking about the implications, some of the possibilities. I *think* we've just been handed the greatest boon a surgeon ever had to work with. Joan, can you see inside a human body?"

"I don't know. I've never—"

"Look at me."

She stared at him for a silent moment. "Why—why, I can see your heart beat! I can see—"

"Phil, can you teach me to see the way she does?"

Huxley rubbed his nose. "I don't know. Maybe—"

Joan bent over the big chair in which the doctor was seated. "Won't he go under, Phil?"

"Hell, no. I've tried everything but tapping his skull with a bungstarter. I don't believe there's any brain there to hypnotize."

"Don't be pettish. Let's try again. How do you feel, Ben?"

"All right, but wide awake."

"I'm going out of the room this time. Maybe I'm a distracting factor. Now be a good boy and go sleepy-bye." She left them.

Five minutes later Huxley called out to her, "Come on back in, kid. He's under."

She came in and looked at Coburn where he law sprawled in her big easy chair, quiet, eyes half closed. "Ready for me?" she asked, turning to Huxley.

"Yes. Get ready." She lay down on the couch. "You know what I want; get in rapport with Ben as soon as you go under. Need any persuasion to get to sleep?"

"No."

"Very well, then—Sleep!"

She became quiet, lax.

"Are you under, Joan?"

"Yes, Phil."

"Can you reach Ben's mind?"

A short pause: "Yes."

"What do you find?"

"Nothing. It's like an empty room, but friendly. Wait a moment—he greeted me."

"What did he say?"

"Just a greeting. It wasn't in words."

"Can you hear me, Ben?"

"Sure, Phil."

"You two are together?"

"Yes. Yes, indeed."

"Listen to me, both of you. I want you to wake up slowly, remaining in rapport. Then Joan is to teach Ben how to perceive that which is not seen. Can you do it?"

"Yes, Phil, we can." It was as if one voice had spoken.

CHAPTER FOUR

HOLIDAY

"FRANKLY, MR. HUXLEY, I can't understand your noncooperative attitude." The President of Western University let the stare from his slightly bulging eyes rest on the second button of Phil's vest. "You have been given every facility for sound useful research along lines of proven worth. Your program of instructing has been kept light in order that you might make use of your undoubted ability. You have been acting chairman of your sub-department this past semester. Yet instead of profiting by your unusual opportunities, you have, by your own admission, been, shall we say, frittering away your time in the childish pursuit of old wives' tales and silly superstitions. Bless me, man, I don't understand it!"

Phil answered, with controlled exasperation, "But Doctor Brinckley, if you would permit me to show you—"

The president interposed a palm. "Please, Mr. Huxley. It is not necessary to go over that ground again. One more thing, it has come to my attention that you have been interfering in the affairs of the medical school."

"The medical school! I haven't set foot inside it in weeks."

"It has come to me from unquestioned authority that you have influenced Doctor Coburn to disregard the advice of the staff diagnosticians in performing surgical operations—the best diagnosticians, let me add, on the West Coast."

Huxley maintained his voice at toneless politeness. "Let us suppose for the moment that I have influenced Doctor Coburn—I do not concede the point—has there been any case in which Coburn's refusal to follow diagnosis has failed to be justified by the subsequent history of the case?"

"That is beside the point. The point is—I can't have my

staff from one school interfering in the affairs of another school. You see the justice of that, I am sure."

"I do not admit that I have interfered. In fact, I deny it."

"I am afraid I shall have to be the judge of that." Brinckley rose from his desk and came around to where Huxley stood. "Now Mr. Huxley—may I call you Philip? I like to have my juniors in our institution think of me as a friend. I want to give you the same advice that I would give to my son. The semester will be over in a day or two. I think you need a vacation. The Board has made some little difficulty over renewing your contract inasmuch as you have not yet completed your doctorate. I took the liberty of assuring them that you would submit a suitable thesis this coming academic year—and I feel sure that you can if you will only devote your efforts to sound, constructive work. You take your vacation, and when you come back you can outline your proposed thesis to me. I am quite sure the Board will make no difficulty about your contract then."

"I had intended to write up the results of my current research for my thesis."

Brinckley's brows raised in polite surprise. "Really? But that is out of the question, my boy, as you know. You do need a vacation. Good-bye then; if I do not see you again before commencement, let me wish you a pleasant holiday now."

When a stout door separated him from the president, Huxley dropped his pretense of good manners and hurried across the campus, ignoring students and professors alike. He found Ben and Joan waiting for him at their favorite bench, looking across the La Brea Tar Pits toward Wilshire Boulevard.

He flopped down on the seat beside them. Neither of the men spoke, but Joan was unable to control her impatience. "Well, Phil? What did the old fossil have to say?"

"Gimme a cigaret." Ben handed him a pack and waited. "He didn't say much—just threatened me with the loss of my job and the ruination of my academic reputation if I didn't knuckle under and be his tame dog—all in the politest of terms of course."

"But Phil, didn't you offer to bring me in and show him the progress you had already made?"

"I didn't bring your name into it; it was useless. He knew who you were well enough—he made a sidelong reference to the inadvisability of young instructors seeing female students socially except under formal, fully chaperoned conditions—talked about the high moral tone of the university, and our obligation to the public!"

"Why, the dirty minded old so-and-so! I'll tear him apart for that!"

"Take it easy, Joan." Ben Coburn's voice was mild and thoughtful. "Just how did he threaten you, Phil?"

"He refused to renew my contract at this time. He intends to keep me on tenterhooks all summer, then if I come back in the fall and make a noise like a rabbit, he might renew—if he feels like it. Damn him! The thing that got me the sorest was a suggestion that I was slipping and needed a rest."

"What are you going to do?"

"Look for a job, I guess. I've got to eat."

"Teaching job?"

"I suppose so, Ben."

"Your chances aren't very good, are they, without a formal release from Western? They can blacklist you pretty effectively. You've actually got about as much freedom in the matter as a professional ballplayer."

Phil looked glum and said nothing. Joan sighed and looked out across the marshy depression surrounding the tar pits. Then she smiled and said, "We could lure old Picklepuss down here and push him in."

Both men smiled but did not answer. Joan muttered to herself something about sissies. Ben addressed Phil. "You know, Phil, the old boy's idea about a vacation wasn't too stupid; I could do with one myself."

"Anything in particular in mind?"

"Why, yes, more or less. I've been out here seven years

34

and never really seen the state. I'd like to start out and drive, with no particular destination in mind. Then we could go on up past Sacramento and into northern California. They say it's magnificent country up there. We could take in the High Sierras and the Big Trees on the way back."

"That certainly sounds inviting."

"You could take along your research notes and we could talk about your ideas as we drove. If you decided you wanted to write up some phase, we could just lay over while you did it."

Phil stuck out his hand. "It's a deal, Ben. When do we start?"

"As soon as the term closes."

"Let's see—we ought to be able to get underway late Friday afternoon then. Which car will we use, yours or mine?"

"My coupe ought to be about right. It has lots of baggage space."

Joan, who had followed the conversation with interest, broke in on them. "Why use your car, Ben? Three people can't be comfortable in a coupe."

"Three people? Wha' d'yu mean, three people? You aren't going, bright eyes."

"So? That's what you think. You can't get rid of me at this point; I'm the laboratory case. Oh no, you can't leave me behind."

"But Joan, this is a stag affair."

"Oh, so you want to get rid of me?"

"Now Joan, we didn't say that. It just would look like the devil for you to be barging about the country with a couple of men—"

"Sissies! Tissyprissies! Pantywaists! Worried about your reputations."

"No, we're not. We're worried about yours."

"It won't wash. No girl who lives alone has any reputation. She can be as pure as Ivory soap and the cats on the campus, both sexes, will take her to pieces anyway. What are you so scared of? We aren't going to cross any state lines."

35

Coburn and Huxley exchanged the secret look that men employ when confronted by the persistence of an unreasonable woman.

"Look out, Joan!" A big red Santa Fe bus took the shoulder on the opposite side of the highway and slithered past. Joan switched the tail of the grey sedan around an oil tanker truck and trailer on their own side of the road before replying. When she did, she turned her head to speak directly to Phil who was riding in the back seat.

"What's the matter, Phil?"

"You darn near brought us into a head on collision with about twenty tons of the Santa Fe's best rolling stock!"

"Don't be nervous; I've been driving since I was sixteen and I've never had an accident."

"I'm not surprised; you'll never have but one. Anyhow," Phil went on, "can't you keep your eyes on the road? That's not too much to ask, is it?"

"I don't need to watch the road. Look." She turned her head far around and showed him that her eyes were jammed shut. The needle of the speedometer hovered around ninety.

"Joan! Please!"

She opened her eyes and faced front once more. "But I don't have to look in order to see. You taught me that yourself, Smarty. Don't you remember?"

"Yes, yes, but I never thought you'd apply it to driving a car!"

"Why not? I'm the safest driver you ever saw; I can see everything that's on the road, even around a blind curve. If I need to, I read the other drivers' minds to see what they are going to do next."

"She's right, Phil. The few times I've paid attention to her driving she's been doing just exactly what I would have done in the same circumstances. That's why I haven't been nervous."

"All right. All right," Phil answered, "but would you two supermen keep in mind that there is a slightly nervous

ordinary mortal in the back seat who can't see around corners?"

"I'll be good," said Joan soberly. "I didn't mean to scare
you, Phil."

"I'm interested," resumed Ben, "in what you said about
not looking toward anything you wanted to see. I can't do
it too satisfactorily. I remember once you said it made you
dizzy to look away and still use direct perception."

"It used to, Ben, but I got over it, and so will you. It's just
a matter of breaking old habits. To me, every direction is in
'front'—all around and up and down. I can focus my attention in any direction, or two or three directions at once. I
can even pick a point off away from where I am physically,
and look at the other side of things—but that is harder."

"You two make me feel like the mother of the Ugly Duck-
ling," said Phil bitterly. "Will you still think of me kindly
when you have passed beyond human communication?"

"Poor Phil!" exclaimed Joan, with sincere sympathy in
her voice. "You taught us, but no one has bothered to teach
you. Tell you what, Ben, let's stop tonight at an auto camp—
pick a nice quiet one on the outskirts of Sacramento—and
spend a couple of days doing for Phil what he has done for
us."

"Okay by me. It's a good idea."

"That's mighty white of you, pardner," Phil conceded,
but it was obvious that he was pleased and mollified. "After
you get through with me will I be able to drive a car on two
wheels, too?"

"Why not learn to levitate?" Ben suggested. "It's simpler—less expensive and nothing to get out of order."

"Maybe we will some day," returned Phil, quite seriously,
"there's no telling where this line of investigation may lead."

"Yeah, you're right," Ben answered him with equal sobri-
ety. "I'm getting so that I can believe seven impossible things
before breakfast. What were you saying just before we passed
that oil tanker?"

"I was just trying to lay before you an idea I've been

mulling over in my mind the past several weeks. It's a big idea, so big that I can hardly believe it myself."

"Well, spill it."

Phil commenced checking points off on his fingers. "We've proved, or tended to prove, that the normal human mind has powers previously unsuspected, haven't we?"

"Tentatively—yes. It looks that way."

"Powers way beyond any that the race as a whole makes regular use of."

"Yes, surely. Go on."

"And we have reason to believe that these powers exist, have their being, by virtue of certain areas of the brain to which functions were not previously assigned by physiologists? That is to say, they have organic basis, just as the eye and the sight centers in the brain are the organic basis for normal sight?"

"Yes, of course."

"You can trace the evolution of any organ from a simple beginning to a complex, highly developed form. The organ develops through use. In an evolutionary sense function begets organ."

"Yes. That's elementary."

"Don't you see what that implies?"

Coburn looked puzzled, then a look of comprehension spread over his face. Phil continued, with delight in his voice, "You see it, too? The conclusion is inescapable: there must have been a time when the entire race used these strange powers as easily as they heard, or saw, or smelled. And there must have been a long, long period—hundreds of thousands, probably millions of years—during which these powers were developed as a race. Individuals couldn't do it, any more than I could grow wings. It had to be done racially, over a long period of time. Mutation theory is no use either—mutation goes by little jumps, with use confirming the change. No indeed—these strange powers are vestigial—hangovers from a time when the whole race had 'em and used 'em."

Phil stopped talking, and Ben did not answer him, but sat

in a brown study while some ten miles spun past. Joan started to speak once, then thought better of it. Finally Ben commenced to speak slowly.

"I can't see any fault in your reasoning. It's not reasonable to assume that whole areas of the brain with complex functions 'jest growed'. But, brother, you've sure raised hell with modern anthropology."

"That worried me when I first got the notion, and that's why I kept my mouth shut. Do you know anything about anthropology?"

"Nothing except the casual glance that any medical student gets."

"Neither did I, but I had quite a lot of respect for it. Professor Whoosistwitchell would reconstruct one of our great grand-daddies from his collar bone and his store teeth and deliver a long dissertation on his most intimate habits, and I would swallow it, hook, line, and sinker, and be much impressed. But I began to read up on the subject. Do you know what I found?"

"Go ahead."

"In the first place there isn't a distinguished anthropologist in the world but what you'll find one equally distinguished who will call him a diamond-studded liar. They can't agree on the simplest elements of their alleged science. In the second place, there isn't a corporal's guard of really decent exhibits to back up their assertions about the ancestry of mankind. I never saw so much stew from one oyster. They write book after book and what have they got to go on?—The Dawson Man, the Pekin Man, the Heidelberg Man and a couple of others. And those aren't complete skeletons, a damaged skull, a couple of teeth, maybe another bone or two."

"Oh now, Phil, there were lots of specimens found of Cro-Magnon men."

"Yes, but they were true men. I'm talking about submen, our evolutionary predecessors. You see, I was trying to prove myself wrong. If man's ascent had been a long steady climb, submen into savages, savages to barbarians, barbarians per-

39

fecting their cultures into civilization . . . all this with only minor setbacks of a few centuries, or a few thousands years at the most . . . and with our present culture the highest the race had ever reached . . . If all that was true, then my idea was wrong.

"You follow me, don't you? The internal evidence of the brain proves that mankind, sometime in its lost history, climbed to heights undreamed of today. In some fashion the race slipped back. And this happened so long ago that we have found no record of it anywhere. These brutish submen, that the anthropologists set such store by, *can't* be our ancestors; they are too new, too primitive, too young. They are too recent; they allow for no time for the race to develop these abilities whose existence we have proved. Either anthropology is all wet, or Joan can't do the things we have seen her do."

The center of the controversy said nothing. She sat at the wheel, as the big car sped along, her eyes closed against the slanting rays of the setting sun, seeing the road with an inner impossible sight.

Five days were spent in coaching Huxley and a sixth on the open road. Sacramento lay far behind them. For the past hour Mount Shasta had been visible from time to time through openings in the trees. Phil brought the car to a stop on a view point built out from the pavement of U.S. Highway 99. He turned to his passengers. "All out, troops," he said. "Catch a slice of scenery."

The three stood and stared over the canyon of the Sacramento River at Mount Shasta, thirty miles away. It was sweater weather and the air was as clear as a child's gaze. The peak was framed by two of the great fir trees which marched down the side of the canyon. Snow still lay on the slopes of the cone and straggled down as far as the timberline.

Joan muttered something. Ben turned his head. "What did you say, Joan?"

"Me? Nothing—I was saying over a bit of poetry to myself."

"What was it?"

"Tietjens' *Most Sacred Mountain:*

" '*Space and the twelve clean winds are here;*
And with them broods eternity—a swift white peace, a presence
manifest.
The rhythm ceases here. Time has no place. This is the end that has
no end'."

Phil cleared his throat and self-consciously broke the silence. "I think I see what you mean."

Joan faced them. "Boys," she stated, "I am going to climb Mount Shasta."

Ben studied her dispassionately. "Joan," he pronounced, "You are full of hop."

"I mean it. I didn't say you were going to—I said I was."

"But we are responsible for your safety and welfare—and I for one don't relish the thought of a fourteen-thousand foot climb."

"You are *not* responsible for my safety; I'm a free citizen. Anyhow a climb wouldn't hurt you any; it would help to get rid of some of that fat you've been storing up against winter."

"Why," inquired Phil, "are you so determined so suddenly to make this climb?"

"It's really not a sudden decision, Phil. Ever since we left Los Angeles I've had a recurring dream that I was climbing, climbing, up to some high place . . . and that I was very happy because of it. Today I know that it was Shasta I was climbing."

"How do you know it?"

"I know it."

"Ben, what do you think?"

The doctor picked up a granite pebble and shied it out in the general direction of the river. He waited for it to come to rest several hundred feet down the slope. "I guess," he said, "we'd better buy some hobnailed boots."

Phil paused and the two behind him on the narrow path

were forced to stop, too. "Joan," he asked, with a worried tone, "is this the way we came?"

They huddled together, icy wind cutting at their faces like rusty blades and gusts of snow eddying about them and stinging their eyes, while Joan considered her answer. "I think so," she ventured at last, "but even with my eyes closed this snow makes everything look different."

"That's my trouble, too. I guess we pulled a boner when we decided against a guide . . . but who would have thought that a beautiful summer day could end up in a snow storm?"

Ben stamped his feet and clapped his hands together. "Let's get going," he urged. "Even if this is the right road, we've got the worst of it ahead of us before we reach the rest cabin. Don't forget that stretch of glacier we crossed."

"I wish I could forget it," Phil answered him soberly. "I don't fancy the prospect of crossing it in this nasty weather."

"Neither do I, but if we stay here we freeze."

With Ben now in the lead they resumed their cautious progress, heads averted to the wind, eyes half closed. Ben checked them again after a couple of hundred yards. "Careful, gang," he warned, "the path is almost gone here, and it's slippery." He went forward a few steps. "It's rather—" They heard him make a violent effort to recover his balance, then fall heavily.

"Ben! Ben!" Phil called out, "are you all right?"

"I guess so," he gasped. "I gave my left leg an awful bang. Be careful."

They saw that he was on the ground, hanging part way over the edge of the path. Cautiously they approached until they were alongside him. "Lend me a hand, Phil. Easy, now."

Phil helped him wiggle back onto the path. "Can you stand up?"

"I'm afraid not. My left leg gave me the devil when I had to move just now. Take a look at it, Phil. No, don't bother to take the boot off; look right through it."

"Of course. I forgot." Phil studied the limb for a moment.

"It's pretty bad, fella—a fracture of the shin bone about four inches below the knee."

Coburn whistled a couple of bars of *Suwannee River*, then said, "Isn't that just too, too lovely? Simple or compound fracture, Phil?"

"Seems like a clean break, Ben."

"Not that it matters much one way or the other just now. What do we do next?"

Joan answered him. "We must build a litter and get you down the mountain!"

"Spoken like a true girl scout, kid. Have you figured how you and Phil can maneuver a litter, with me in it, over that stretch of ice?"

"We'll *have* to—somehow." But her voice lacked confidence.

"It won't work, kid. You two will have to straighten me out and bed me down, then go on down the mountain and stir out a rescue party with proper equipment. I'll get some sleep while you're gone. I'd appreciate it if you'd leave me some cigarets."

"No!" Joan protested. "We won't leave you here alone."

Phil added his objections. "Your plan is as bad as Joan's, Ben. It's all very well to talk about sleeping until we get back, but you know as well as I do that you would die of exposure if you spent a night like this on the ground with no protection."

"I'll just have to chance it. What better plan can you suggest?"

"Wait a minute. Let me think." He sat down on the ledge beside his friend and pulled at his left ear. "This is the best I can figure out: We'll have to get you to some place that is a little more sheltered, and build a fire to keep you warm. Joan can stay with you and keep the fire going while I go down after help."

"That's all right," put in Joan, "except that I will be the one to go after help. You couldn't find your way in the dark and the snow, Phil. You know yourself that your direct perception isn't reliable as yet—you'd get lost."

Both men protested. "Joan, you're not going to start off alone."—"We can't permit that, Joan."

"That's a lot of gallant nonsense. Of course I'm going."

"No." It was a duet.

"Then we all stay here tonight, and huddle around a fire. I'll go down in the morning."

"That might do," Ben conceded, "if—"

"Good evening, friends." A tall, elderly man stood on the ledge behind them. Steady blue eyes regarded them from under shaggy white eyebrows. He was smooth shaven but a mane of white hair matched the eyebrows. Joan thought he looked like Mark Twain.

Coburn recovered first. "Good evening," he answered, "if it is a good evening—which I doubt."

The stranger smiled with his eyes. "My name is Ambrose, ma'am. But your friend is in need of some assistance. If you will permit me, sir—" He knelt down and examined Ben's leg, without removing the boot. Presently he raised his head. "This will be somewhat painful. I suggest, son, that you go to sleep." Ben smiled at him, closed his eyes, and gave evidence by his slow, regular breathing that he was asleep.

The man who called himself Ambrose slipped away into the shadows. Joan tried to follow him with perception, but this she found curiously hard to do. He returned in a few minutes with several straight sticks which he broke to a uniform length of about twenty inches. These he proceeded to bind firmly to Ben's left shin with a roll of cloth which he had removed from his trouser pocket.

When he was satisfied that the primitive splint was firm, he picked Coburn up in his arms, handling the not inconsiderable mass as if it were a child. "Come," he said.

They followed him without a word, back the way they had come, single file through the hurrying snowflakes. Five hundred yards, six hundred yards, then he took a turn that had not been on the path followed by Joan and the two men,

44

and strode confidently away in the gloom. Joan noticed that he was wearing a light cotton shirt with neither coat nor sweater, and wondered that he had come so far with so little protection against the weather. He spoke to her over his shoulder,

"I like cold weather, ma'am."

He walked between two large boulders, apparently disappeared into the side of the mountain. They followed him and found themselves in a passageway which led diagonally into the living rock. They turned a corner and were in an octagonal living room, high ceilinged and panelled in some mellow, light-colored wood. It was softly illuminated by indirect lighting, but possessed no windows. One side of the octagon was a fireplace with a generous hearth in which a wood fire burned hospitably. There was no covering on the flagged floor, but it was warm to the feet.

The old man paused with his burden and indicated the comfortable fittings of the room—three couches, old-fashioned heavy chairs, a chaise longue—with a nod. "Be seated, friends, and make yourselves comfortable. I must see that your companion is taken care of, then we will find refreshment for you." He went out through a door opposite the one by which they had entered, still carrying Coburn in his arms.

Phil looked at Joan and Joan looked at Phil. "Well," he said, "what do you make of it?"

"I think we've found a 'home from home'. This is pretty swell."

"What do we do next?"

"I'm going to pull that chaise longue up to the fire, take off my boots, and get my feet warm and my clothes dry."

When Ambrose returned ten minutes later he found them blissfully toasting their tired feet before the fire. He was bearing a tray from which he served them big steaming bowls of onion soup, hard rolls, apple pie, and strong black tea. While doing so he stated, "Your friend is resting. There is no need to see him until tomorrow. When you have eaten, you will find sleeping rooms in the passageway, with what you need for your immediate comfort." He indicated the door from which he had just come. "No chance to mistake them; they are the lighted rooms immediately at hand. I bid you goodnight now." He picked up the tray and turned to leave.

"Oh, I say," began Phil hesitantly, "This is awfully good of you, Mister, uh—"

"You are very welcome, sir. Bierce is my name. Ambrose Bierce. Goodnight." And he was gone.

CHAPTER FIVE

"—THROUGH A GLASS, DARKLY"

WHEN PHIL ENTERED the living room the next morning he found a small table set with a very sound breakfast for three. While he was lifting plate covers and wondering whether good manners required him to wait until joined by others, Joan entered the room. He looked up.

"Oh! It's you. Good morning, and stuff. They set a proper table here. Look." He lifted a plate cover. "Did you sleep well?"

"Like a corpse." She joined his investigations. "They do understand food, don't they? When do we start?"

"When number three gets here, I guess. Those aren't the clothes you had on last night."

"Like it?" She turned around slowly with a swaying mannequin walk. She had on a pearl grey gown that dropped to her toes. It was high waisted; two silver cords crossed between her breasts and encircled her waist, making a girdle. She was shod in silver sandals. There was an air of ancient days about the whole costume.

"It's swell. Why is it a girl always look prettier in simple clothes?"

"Simple—hmmf! If you can buy this for three hundred dollars on Wilshire Boulevard, I'd like to have the address of the shop."

"Hello, troops." Ben stood in the doorway. They both stared at him. "What's the trouble?"

Phil ran his eye down Ben's frame. "How's your leg, Ben?"

"I wanted to ask you about that. How long have I been out? The leg's all well. Wasn't it broken after all?"

"How about it, Phil?" Joan seconded. "You examined it—I didn't."

Phil pulled his ear. "It was broken—or I've gone completely screwy. Let's have a look at it."

Ben was dressed in pajamas and bathrobe. He slid up the pajama leg, and exposed a shin that was pink and healthy. He pounded it with his fist. "See that? Not even a bruise."

"Hmm—You haven't been out long, Ben. Just since last night. Maybe ten or eleven hours."

"Huh?"

"That's right."

"Impossible."

"Maybe so. Let's eat breakfast."

They ate in thoughtful silence, each under pressing necessity of taking stock and reaching some reasonable reorientation. Toward the end of the meal they all happened to look up at once. Phil broke the silence,

"Well . . . How about it?"

"I've just doped it out," volunteered Joan. "We all died in the snow storm and went to Heaven. Pass the marmalade, will you, please?"

"That can't be right," objected Phil, as he complied, "else Ben wouldn't be here. He led a sinful life. But seriously, things have happened which require explanation. Let's tick 'em off: One; Ben breaks a leg last night, it's all healed this morning."

"Wait a minute—are we sure he broke his leg?"

"I'm sure. Furthermore, our host acted as if he thought so too—else why did he bother to carry him? Two; our host has direct perception, or an uncanny knowledge of the mountainside."

"Speaking of direct perception," said Joan, "have either of you tried to look around you and size up the place?"

"No, why?"—"Neither have I."

"Don't bother to. I tried, and it can't be done. I can't perceive past the walls of the room."

"Hmm—we'll put that down as point three. Four; our host says that his name is Ambrose Bierce. Does he mean that he is *the* Ambrose Bierce? You know who Ambrose Bierce was, Joan?"

"Of course I do—I got eddication. He disappeared sometime before I was born."

"That's right—at the time of the outbreak of the first World War. If this is the same man, he must be over a hundred years old."

"He didn't look that old by forty years."

"Well, we'll put it down for what it's worth. Point five;— We'll make this one an omnibus point—why does our host live up here? How come this strange mixture of luxury hotel and cliff dwellers cave anyhow? How can one old man run such a joint? Say, have either of you seen anyone else around the place?"

"I haven't," said Ben. "Someone woke me, but I think it was Ambrose."

"I have," offered Joan. "It was a woman who woke me. She offered me this dress."

"Mrs. Bierce, maybe?"

"I don't think so—she wasn't more than thirty-five. I didn't really get acquainted—she was gone before I was wide awake."

Phil looked from Joan to Ben. "Well, what have we got? Add it up and give us an answer."

"Good morning, young friends!" It was Bierce, standing in the doorway, his rich, virile voice resounding around the many-sided room. The three started as if caught doing something improper.

Coburn recovered first. He stood up and bowed. "Good morning, sir. I believe that you saved my life. I hope to be able to show my gratitude."

Bierce bowed formally. "What service I did I enjoyed doing, sir. I hope that you are all rested?"

"Yes, thank you, and pleasantly filled from your table."

"That is good. Now, if I may join you, we can discuss what you wish to do next. Is it your pleasure to leave, or may we hope to have your company for a while longer?"

"I suppose," said Joan, rather nervously, "that we should get started down as soon as possible. How is the weather?"

"The weather is fair, but you are welcome to remain here as long as you like. Perhaps you would like to see the rest of our home and meet the other members of our household?"

"Oh, I think that would be lovely!"

"It will be my pleasure, ma'am."

"As a matter of fact, Mr. Bierce—" Phil leaned forward a little, his face and manner serious. "—we are quite anxious to see more of your place here and to know more about you. We were speaking of it when you came in."

"Curiosity is natural and healthy. Please ask any question you wish."

"Well—" Phil plunged in. "Ben had a broken leg last night. Or didn't he? It's well this morning."

"He did indeed have a broken leg. It was healed in the night."

Coburn cleared his throat. "Mr. Bierce, my name is Coburn. I am a physician and surgeon, but my knowledge does not extend to such healing as that. Will you tell me more about it?"

"Certainly. You are familiar with regeneration as practiced by the lower life forms. The principle used is the same, but it is consciously controlled by the will and the rate of healing is accelerated. I placed you in hypnosis last night, then surrendered control to one of our surgeons who directed your mind in exerting its own powers to heal its body."

Coburn looked baffled. Bierce continued, "There is really nothing startling about it. The mind and will have always the possibility of complete domination over the body. Our operator simply directs your will to master its body. The technique is simple; you may learn it, if you wish. I assure you that to learn it is easier than to explain it in our cumbersome and imperfect language. I spoke of mind and will as if they were separate. Language forced me to that ridiculous misstatement. There is neither mind, nor will, as entities; there is only—" His voice stopped. Ben felt a blow

ithin his mind like the shock of a sixteen inch rifle, yet it
as painless and gentle. What ever it was, it was as alive as
hummingbird, or a struggling kitten, yet it was calm and
ntroubled.

He saw Joan nodding her head in agreement, her eyes on
ierce.

Bierce went on in his gentle, resonant voice. "Was there
ny other matter troubling any of you?"

"Why, yes, Mr. Bierce," replied Joan, "several things.
What is this place where we are?"

"It is my home, and the home of several of my friends.
ou will understand more about us as you become better
cquainted with us."

"Thank you. It is difficult for me to understand how such
community could exist on this mountaintop without it
eing a matter of common knowledge."

"We have taken certain precautions, ma'am, to avoid
otoriety. Our reasons, and the precautions they inspired
ill become evident to you."

"One more question; this is rather personal; you may
nore it if you like. Are you the Ambrose Bierce who dis-
ppeared a good many years ago?"

"I am. I first came up here in 1880 in search of a cure for
sthma. I retired here in 1914 because I wished to avoid
irect contact with the tragic world events which I saw com-
g and was powerless to stop." He spoke with some reluct-
nce, as if the subject were distasteful, and turned the
onversation. "Perhaps you would like to meet some of my
iends now?"

The apartments extended for a hundred yards along the
ce of the mountain and for unmeasured distances into the
ountain. The thirty-odd persons in residence were far from
owded; there were many rooms not in use. In the course
the morning Bierce introduced them to most of the inhabi-
nts.

They seemed to be of all sorts and ages and of several

nationalities. Most of them were occupied in one way, o
another, usually with some form of research, or with creativ
art. At least Bierce assured them in several cases that researc
was in progress—cases in which no apparatus, no recordin
device, nothing was evident to indicate scientific research.

Once they were introduced to a group of three, two wome
and a man, who were surrounded by the physical evidenc
of their work—biological research. But the circumstanc
were still confusing; two of the trio sat quietly by, doin
nothing, while the third labored at a bench. Bierce explaine
that they were doing some delicate experiments in the po
sibility of activating artificial colloids. Ben inquired,

"Are the other two observing the work?"

Bierce shook his head. "Oh, no. They are all three engage
actively in the work, but at this particular stage they find
expedient to let three brains in rapport direct one set
hands."

Rapport, it developed, was the usual method of collab
oration. Bierce had led them into a room occupied by s
persons. One or two of them looked up and nodded, but d
not speak. Bierce motioned for the three to come away. "The
were engaged in a particularly difficult piece of reconstru
tion; it would not be polite to disturb them."

"But Mr. Bierce," Phil commented, "two of them we
playing chess."

"Yes. They did not need that part of their brains, so the
left it out of rapport. Nevertheless they were very busy."

It was easier to see what the creative artists were doin
In two instances, however, their methods were startlin
Bierce had taken them to the studio of a little gnome of
man, a painter in oil, who was introduced simply as Charle
He seemed glad to see them and chatted vivaciously, witho
ceasing his work. He was doing, with meticulous realism b
with a highly romantic effect, a study of a young girl dancin
a wood nymph, against a pine forest background.

The young people each made appropriate appreciati
comments, Coburn commented that it was remarkable th

he should be able to be so accurate in his anatomical detail without the aid of a model.

"But I have a model," he answered. "She was here last week. See?" He glanced toward the empty model's throne. Coburn and his companions followed the glance, and saw, poised on the throne, a young girl, obviously the model for the picture, frozen in the action of the painting. She was as real as bread and butter.

Charles glanced away. The model's throne was again vacant.

The second instance was not so dramatic, but still less comprehensible. They had met, and chatted with, a Mrs. Draper, a comfortable, matronly soul, who knitted and rocked as they talked. After they had left her Phil inquired about her.

"She is possibly our most able and talented artist," Bierce told him.

"In what field?"

Bierce's shaggy eyebrows came together as he chose his words. "I don't believe I can tell you adequately at this time. She composes moods—arranges emotional patterns in harmonic sequences. It's our most advanced and our most completely human form of art, and yet, until you have experienced it, it is very difficult for me to tell you about it."

"How is it possible to *arrange* emotions?"

"Your great grandfather no doubt thought it impossible to record music. We have a technique for it. You will understand later."

"Is Mrs. Draper the only one who does this?"

"Oh, no. Most of us try our hand at it. It's our favorite art form. I work at it myself but my efforts aren't popular—too gloomy."

The three talked it over that night in the living room they had first entered. This suite had been set aside for their use, and Bierce had left them with the simple statement that he would call on them on the morrow.

53

They felt a pressing necessity to exchange views, and yet each was reluctant to express opinion. Phil broke the silence.

"What kind of people are these? They make me feel as if I were a child who had wandered in where adults were working, but that they were too polite to put me out."

"Speaking of working—there's something odd about the way they work. I don't mean what it is they do—that's odd, too, but it's something else, something about their attitude, or the tempo at which they work."

"I know what you mean, Ben,' Joan agreed, "they are busy all the time, and yet they act as if they had all eternity to finish it. Bierce was like that when he was strapping up your leg. They never hurry." She turned to Phil. "What are you frowning about?"

"I don't know. There is something else we haven't mentioned yet. They have a lot of special talents, sure, but we three know something about special talents—that ought not to confuse us. But there is something else about them that is *different*."

The other two agreed with him but could offer no help. Sometime later Joan said that she was going to bed and left the room. The two men stayed for a last cigaret.

Joan stuck her head back in the room. "I know what it is that is so different about these people," she announced,—"They are so *alive*."

CHAPTER SIX

ICHABOD!

PHILIP HUXLEY WENT TO BED and to sleep as usual. From there on nothing was usual.

He became aware that he was inhabiting another's body, thinking with another's mind. The Other was aware of Huxley, but did not share Huxley's thoughts.

The Other was at home, a home never experienced by Huxley, yet familiar. It was on Earth, incredibly beautiful, each tree and shrub fitting into the landscape as if placed there in the harmonic scheme of an artist. The house grew out of the ground.

The Other left the house with his wife and prepared to leave for the capital of the planet. Huxley thought of the destination as a "capital" yet he knew that the idea of government imposed by force was foreign to the nature of these people. The "capital" was merely the accustomed meeting place of the group whose advice was followed in matters affecting the entire race.

The Other and his wife, accompanied by Huxley's awareness, stepped into the garden, shot straight up into the air, and sped over the countryside, flying hand in hand. The country was green, fertile, parklike, dotted with occasional buildings, but nowhere did Huxley see the jammed masses of a city.

They passed rapidly over a large body of water, perhaps as large as the modern Mediterranean, and landed in a clearing in a grove of olive trees.

The Young Men—so Huxley thought of them—demanded a sweeping change in custom, first, that the ancient knowledge should henceforth be the reward of ability rather than

55

common birthright, and second, that the greater should rule the lesser. Loki urged their case, his arrogant face upthrust and crowned with bright red hair. He spoke in words, a method which disturbed Huxley's host, telepathic rapport being the natural method of mature discussion. But Loki had closed his mind to it.

Jove answered him, speaking for all:

"My son, your words seem vain and without serious meaning. We can not tell your true meaning, for you and your brothers have decided to shut your minds to us. You ask that the ancient knowledge be made the reward of ability. Has it not always been so? Does our cousin, the ape, fly through the air? Is not the infant soul bound by hunger, and sleep, and the ills of the flesh? Can the oriole level the mountain with his glance? The powers of our kind that set us apart from the younger spirits on this planet are now exercised by those who possess the ability, and none other. How can we make that so which is already so?

"You demand that the greater shall rule the lesser. Is it not so now? Has it not always been so? Are you ordered about by the babe at the breast? Does the waving of the grass cause the wind? What dominion do you desire other than over yourself? Do you wish to tell your brother when to sleep and when to eat? If so, to what purpose?"

Vulcan broke in while the old man was still speaking. Huxley felt a stir of shocked repugnance go through the council at this open disregard of good manners.

"Enough of this playing with words. We know what we want; you know what we want. We are determined to take it, council or no. We are sick of this sheeplike existence. We are tired of this sham equality. We intend to put an end to it. We are the strong and the able, the natural leaders of mankind. The rest shall follow us and serve us, as is the natural order of things."

Jove's eyes rested thoughtfully on Vulcan's crooked leg. "You should let me heal that twisted limb, my son."

"No one can heal my limb!"

"No. No one but yourself. And until you heal the twist in your mind, you can not heal the twist in your limb."

"There is no twist in my mind!"

"Then heal your limb."

The young man stirred uneasily. They could see that Vulcan was making a fool of himself. Mercury separated himself from the group and came forward.

"Hear me, Father. We do not purpose warring with you. Rather it is our intention to add to your glory. Declare yourself king under the sun. Let us be your legates to extend your rule to every creature that walks, or crawls, or swims. Let us create for you the pageantry of dominion, the glory of conquest. Let us conserve the ancient knowledge for those who understand it, and provide instead for lesser beings the drama they need. There is no reason why every way should be open to everyone. Rather, if the many serve the few, then will our combined efforts speed us faster on our way, to the profit of master and servant alike. Lead us, Father! Be our King!"

Slowly the elder man shook his head. "Not so. There is no knowledge, other than knowledge of oneself, and that should be to every man who has the wit to learn. There is no power, other than the power to rule oneself, and that can be neither given, nor taken away. As for the poetry of empire, that has all been done before. There is no need to do it again. If such romance amuses you, enjoy it in the records—there is no need to bloody the planet again."

"That is the final word of the council, Father?"

"That is our final word." He stood up and gathered his robe about him, signifying that the session had ended. Mercury shrugged his shoulders and joined his fellows.

There was one more session of the council—the last—called to decide what to do about the ultimatum of the Young Men. Not every member of the council thought alike; they were as diverse as many group of human beings. They *were* human beings—not supermen. Some held out for opposing the Young Men with all the forces at their command—translate them to another dimension, wipe their minds clean, even crush them by major force.

But to use force on the Young Men was contrary to their whole philosophy. "Free will is the primary good of the Cosmos. Shall we degrade, destroy, all that we have worked for by subverting the will of even one man?"

Huxley became aware that these Elders had no need to remain on Earth. They were anxious to move on to another place, the nature of which escaped Huxley, save that it was not of the time and space he knew.

The issue was this: Had they done what they could to help the incompletely developed balance of the race? Were they justified in abdicating?

The decision was yes, but a female member of the council, whose name, it seemed to Huxley, was Demeter, argued that records should be left to help those who survived the inevitable collapse. "It is true that each member of the race must make himself strong, must make himself wise. We cannot make them wise. Yet, after famine and war and hatred have stalked the earth, should there not be a message, telling them of their heritage?"

The council agreed, and Huxley's host, recorder for the council, was ordered to prepare records and to leave them for those who would come after. Jove added an injunction:

"Bind the force patterns so that they shall not dissipate while this planet endures. Place them where they will outlast any local convulsions of the crust, so that some at least will carry down through time."

So ended that dream. But Huxley did not wake—he started at once to dream another dream, not through the eyes of another, but rather as if he watched a stereo-movie, every scene of which was familiar to him.

The first dream, for all its tragic content, had not affected him tragically; but throughout the second dream he was oppressed by a feeling of heartbreak and overpowering weariness.

After the abdication of the Elders, the Young Men carried

58

out their purpose, they established their rule. By fire and sword, searing rays and esoteric forces, chicanery and deception. Convinced of their destiny to rule, they convinced themselves that the end justified the means.

The end was empire—Mu, mightiest of empires and mother of empires.

Huxley saw her in her prime and felt almost that the Young Men had been right—for she was glorious! The heart-choking magnificence filled his eyes with tears; he mourned for the glory, the beautiful breathtaking glory that was hers, and is no more.

Gargantuan silent liners in her skies, broadbeamed vessels at her wharves, loaded with grain and hides and spices, procession of priest and acolyte and humble believer, pomp and pageantry of power—he saw her intricate patterns of beauty and mourned her passing.

But in her swelling power there was decay. Inevitably Atlantis, her richest colony, grew to political maturity and was irked by subordinate status. Schism and apostasy, disaffection and treason, brought harsh retaliation—and new rebellion.

Rebellions rose, were crushed. At last one rose that was not crushed. In less than a month two-thirds of the people of the globe were dead; the remainder were racked by disease and hunger, and left with germ plasm damaged by the forces they had loosed.

But priests still held the ancient knowledge.

Not priests secure in mind and proud of their trust, but priests hunted and fearful, who had seen their hierarchy totter. There were such priests on both sides—and they unchained forces compared with which the previous fighting had been gentle.

The forces disturbed the isostatic balance of the earth's crust.

Mu shuddered and sank some two thousand feet. Tidal waves met at her middle, broke back, surged twice around

59

the globe, climbed the Chinese plains, lapped the feet of Alta Himalaya.

Atlantis shook and rumbled and split for three days before the water covered it. A few escaped by air, to land on ground still wet with the ooze of exposed seabottom, or on peaks high enough to fend off the tidal waves. There they had still to wring a living from the bare soil, with minds unused to primitive art—but some survived.

Of Mu there was not a trace. As for Atlantis, a few islands, mountaintops short days before, marked the spot. Waters rolled over the twin Towers of the Sun and fish swam through the gardens of the viceroy.

The woebegone feeling which had pursued Huxley now overwhelmed him. He seemed to hear a voice in his head:

"Woe! Cursed be Loki! Cursed be Venus! Cursed be Vulcan! Thrice cursed am I, their apostate servant, Orab, Archpriest of the Isles of the Blessed. Woe is me! Even as I curse I long for Mu, mighty and sinful. Twenty-one years ago, seeking a place to die, on this mountaintop I stumbled on this record of the mighty ones who were before us. Twenty-one years I have labored to make the record complete, searching the dim recesses of my mind for knowledge long unused, roaming the other planes for knowledge I never had. Now in the eight hundred and ninety-second year of my life, and of the destruction of Mu the three hundred and fifth, I, Orab, return to my fathers."

Huxley was very happy to wake up.

CHAPTER SEVEN

"THE FATHERS HAVE EATEN SOUR GRAPES, AND THE CHILDREN'S TEETH ARE SET ON EDGE."

BEN WAS IN THE LIVING ROOM when Phil came in to breakfast. Joan arrived almost on Phil's heels. There were shadows under her eyes and she looked unhappy. Ben spoke in a tone that was almost surly.

"What's troubling you, Joan? You look like the wrath to come."

"Please, Ben," she answered, in a tired voice, "don't heckle me. I've had bad dreams all night."

"That so? Sorry—but if you think you had bad dreams all night, you should have seen the cute little nightmares I've been riding."

Phil looked at the two of them. "Listen—have you both had odd dreams all night?"

"Wasn't that what we were just saying?" Ben sounded exasperated.

"What did you dream about?"

Neither one answered him.

"Wait a minute. I had some very strange dreams myself." He pulled his notebook out of a pocket and tore out three sheets. "I want to find out something. Will you each write down what your dreams were about, before anyone says anything more? Here's a pencil, Joan."

They balked a little, but complied.

"Read them aloud, Joan."

She picked up Ben's slip and read, " 'I dreamed that your theory about the degeneracy of the human race was perfectly correct.' "

She put it down and picked up Phil's slip. " 'dreamt that

I was present at the Twilight of the Gods, and that I saw the destruction of Mu and Atlantis.' "

There was dead silence as she took the last slip, her own.

"My dream was about how the people destroyed themselves by rebelling against Odin."

Ben was first to commit himself. "Anyone of those slips could have applied to my dreams." Joan nodded. Phil got up again, went out, and returned at once with his diary. He opened it and handed it to Joan.

"Kid, will you read that aloud—starting with 'June sixteenth'?"

She read it through slowly, without looking up from the pages. Phil waited until she had finished and closed the book before speaking. "Well," he said, "well?"

Ben crushed out a cigaret which had burned down to his fingers. "It's a remarkably accurate description of my dream, except that the elder you call Jove, I thought of as Ahuramazda."

"And I thought Loki was Lucifer."

"You're both right," agreed Phil. "I don't remember any spoken names for any of them. It just seemed that I knew what their names were."

"Me, too."

"Say," interjected Ben, "we are talking as if these dreams were real—as if we had all been to the same movie."

Phil turned on him. "Well, what do *you* think?"

"Oh, the same as you do, I guess. I'm stumped. Does anybody mind if I eat breakfast—or drink some coffee, at least?"

Bierce came in before they had a chance to talk it over after breakfast—by tacit consent they had held their tongues during a sketchy meal.

"Good morning, ma'am. Good morning, gentlemen."

"Good morning, Mr. Bierce."

"I see," he said, searching their faces, "that none of you look very happy this morning. That is not surprising; no one does immediately after experiencing the records."

Ben pushed back his chair and leaned across the table at Bierce. "Those dreams were deliberately arranged for us?"

"Yes, indeed—but we were sure that you were ready to profit by them. But I have come to ask you to interview the Senior. If you can hold your questions for him, it will be simpler."

"The Senior?"

"You haven't met him as yet. It is the way we refer to the one we judge best fitted to co-ordinate our activities."

Ephraim Howe had the hills of New England in his face, lean gnarled cabinet-maker's hands. He was not young. There was courtly grace in his lanky figure. Everything about him— the twinkle in his pale blue eyes, the clasp of his hand, his drawl—bespoke integrity.

"Sit yourselves down," he said, "I'll come straight to the point"—he called it 'pint.' "You've been exposed to a lot of curious things and you've a right to know why. You've seen the Ancient Records now—part of 'em. I'll tell you how this institution came about, what it's for, and why you are going to be asked to join us.

"Wait a minute. Waaaait a minute," he added, holding up a hand. "Don't say anything just yet . . .."

When Fra Junipero Serra first laid eyes on Mount Shasta in 1781, the Indians told him it was a holy place, only for medicine men. He assured them that he was a medicine man, serving a greater Master, and to keep face, dragged his sick, frail old body up to the snow line, where he slept before returning.

The dream he had there—of the Garden of Eden, the Sin, the Fall, and the Deluge—convinced him that it was indeed a holy place. He returned to San Francisco, planning to found a mission at Shasta. But there was too much for one old man to do—so many souls to save, so many mouths to feed. He surrendered his soul to rest two years later, but laid an injunction on a fellow monk to carry out his intention.

It is recorded that this friar left the northernmost mission in 1785 and did not return.

The Indians fed the holy man who lived on the mountain until 1843, by which time he had gathered about him a group of neophytes, three Indians, a Russian, a Yankee mountainman. The Russian carried on after the death of the friar until joined by a Chinese, fled from his indenture. The Chinese made more progress in a few weeks than the Russian had in half of a lifetime; the Russian gladly surrendered first place to him.

The Chinese was still there over a hundred years later, though long since retired from administration. He tutored in esthetics and humor.

"And this establishment has just one purpose," continued Ephraim Howe. "We aim to see to it that Mu and Atlantis don't happen again. Everything that the Young Men stood for, we are against.

"We see the history of the world as a series of crises in a conflict between two opposing philosophies. Ours is based on the notion that life, consciousness, intelligence, ego is the important thing in the world." For an instant only he touched them telepathically; they felt again the vibrantly alive thing that Ambrose Bierce had showed them and been unable to define in words. "That puts us in conflict with every force that tends to destroy, deaden, degrade the human spirit, or to make it act contrary to its nature. We see another crisis approaching; we need recruits. You've been selected.

"This crisis has been growing on us since Napoleon. Europe has gone, and Asia—surrendered to authoritarianism, nonsense like the 'leader principle,' totalitarianism, all the bonds placed on liberty which treat men as so many economic and political units with no importance as individuals. No dignity—do what you're told, believe what you are told, and shut your mouth! Workers, soldiers, breeding units . . .

"If *that* were the object of life, there would have been no point in including consciousness in the scheme at all!

"This continent," Howe went on, "has been a refuge of

freedom, a place where the soul could grow. But the forces that killed enlightenment in the rest of the world are spreading here. Little by little they have whittled away at human liberty and human dignity. A repressive law, a bullying school board, a blind dogma to be accepted under pain of persecution—doctrines that will shackle men and put blinders on their eyes so that they will never regain their lost heritage.

"We need help to fight it."

Huxley stood up. "You can count on us."

Before Joan and Coburn could speak the Senior interposed. "Don't answer yet. Go back to your chambers and think about it. Sleep on it. We'll talk again."

CHAPTER EIGHT

"PRECEPT UPON PRECEPT . . ."

HAD THE PLACE ON MOUNT SHASTA been a university and possessed a catalog (which it did not), the courses offered therein might have included the following:

TELEPATHY. Basic course required of all students not qualified by examination. Practical instruction up to and including rapport. Prerequisite in all departments. Laboratory.

RATIOCINATION, I, II, III, IV. R.I. Memory. R.II. Perception; clairvoyance, clairaudience, discretion of mass, -time, -and-space, non-mathematical relation, order, and structure, harmonic form and interval.
R.III. Dual and parallel thought processes. Detachment.
R.IV. Meditation (seminar)

AUTOKINETICS. Discrete kinesthesia. Endocrine control with esp. application to the affective senses and to suppression of fatigue, regeneration, transformation (clinical aspects of lycanthropy), sex determination, inversion, autoanaesthesia, rejuvenation.

TELEKINETICS. Life-mass-space-time continua. Prerequisite; autokinetics. Teleportation and general action at a distance. Projection. Dynamics. Statics. Orientation.

HISTORY. Courses by arrangement. Special discussions of psychometry with reference to telepathic records, and of metempsychosis. Evaluation is a prerequisite for all courses in this department.

HUMAN ESTHETICS. Seminar. Autokinetics and technique of telepathic recording (psychometry) a prerequisite.

HUMAN ETHICS. Seminar. Given concurrently with all other courses. Consult with instructor.

Perhaps some of the value of the instruction would have been lost had it been broken up into disjointed courses as outlined above. In any case the adepts on Mount Shasta could and did instruct in all these subjects. Huxley, Coburn, and Joan Freeman learned from tutors who led them to teach themselves, and they took it as an eel seeks the sea, with a sense of returning home after a long absence.

All three made rapid progress; being possessed of rudimentary perception and some knowledge of telepathy, their instructors could teach them directly. First they learned to control their bodies. They regained the control over each function, each muscle, each tissue, each gland, that a man should possess, but has largely forgotten—save a few obscure students in the far east. There was a deep, welling delight in willing the body to obey and having it comply. They became intimately aware of their bodies, but their bodies no longer tyrannized them. Fatigue, hunger, cold, pain—these things no longer drove them, but rather were simply useful signals that a good engine needed attention.

Nor did the engine need as much attention as before; the body was driven by a mind that knew precisely both the capacity and its limitations. Furthermore, through understanding their bodies, they were enabled to increase those capacities to their full potential. A week of sustained activity, without rest, or food, or water, was as easy as a morning's work had been. As for mental labor, it did not cease at all, save when they willed it—despite sleep, digestive languor, ennui, external stimuli, or muscular activity.

The greatest delight was levitation.

To fly through the air, to hang suspended in the quiet heart of a cloud, to sleep, like Mohamet, floating between ceiling and floor—these were sensuous delights unexpected, and never before experienced, except in dreams, dimly. Joan in particular drank this new joy with lusty abandon. Once she remained away two days, never setting foot to ground, sharing the sky and wind and swallow, the icy air of the heights smoothing her bright body. She dove and soared, looped and spiralled, and dropped, a dead weight, knees drawn up to forehead, from stratosphere to treetop.

During the night she paced a transcontinental plane, flying unseen above it for a thousand miles. When she grew bored with this, she pressed her face for a moment against the one lighted port of the plane, and looked inside. The startled wholesale merchant who stared back into her eyes thought that he had been vouchsafed a glimpse of an angel. He went promptly from the airport of his destination to the office of his lawyer, who drew up for him a will establishing scholarships for divinity students.

Huxley found it difficult to learn to levitate. His inquiring mind demanded a reason why the will should apparently be able to set at naught the inexorable "law" of gravitation, and his doubt dissipated his volition. His tutor reasoned with him patiently.

"You know that intangible will can affect the course of mass in the continuum; you experience it whenever you move your hand. Are you powerless to move your hand because you can not give a full rational explanation of the mystery? Life has power to affect matter; you know that—you have experienced it directly. It is a fact. Now there is no 'why' about any fact in the unlimited sense in which you ask the question. There it stands, serene, demonstrating itself. One may observe relations between facts, the relations being other facts, but to pursue those relations back to final meanings is not possible to a mind which is itself relative. First you tell me *why* you *are* . . . then I will tell you why levitation is possible.

"Now come," he continued, place yourself in rapport with me, and try to feel how I do, as I levitate."

Phil tried again. "I don't get it," he concluded miserably.

"Look down."

Phil did so, gasped, and fell three feet to the floor. That night he joined Ben and Joan in a flight over the High Sierras.

Their tutor enjoyed with quiet amusement the zest with

which they entered into the sport made possible by the newly acquired mastery of their bodies. He knew that their pleasure was natural and healthy, suited to their stage of development, and he knew that they would soon learn, of themselves, its relative worth, and then be ready to turn their minds to more serious work.

"Oh, no, Brother Junipero wasn't the only man to stumble on the records," Charles assured them, talking as he painted. "You must have noticed how high places have significance in the religions of every race. Some of them must be repositories of the ancient records."

"Don't you know for certain?" asked Phil.

"Indeed yes, in many cases—Alta Himalaya, for example. I was speaking of what an intelligent man might infer from matters of common knowledge. Consider how many mountains are of prime importance in as many different religions. Mount Olympus, Popocatepetl, Mauna Loa, Everest, Sinai, Tai Shan, Ararat, Fujiyama, several places in the Andes. And in every religion there are accounts of a teacher bringing back inspired messages from high places—Gautama, Jesus, Joseph Smith, Confucius, Moses. They all come down from high places and tell stories of creation, and downfall, and redemption.

"Of all the old accounts the best is found in Genesis. Making allowance for the fact that it was first written in the language of uncivilized nomads, it is an exact, careful account."

Huxley poked Coburn in the ribs. "How do you like that, my skeptical friend?" Then to Charles, "Ben has been a devout atheist since he first found out that Santa Claus wore false whiskers; it hurts him to have his fondest doubts overturned."

Coburn grinned, unperturbed. "Take it easy, son. I can express my own doubts, unassisted. You've brought to mind another matter, Charles. Some of these mountains don't seem old enough to have been used for the ancient records—

Shasta, for example. It's volcanic and seems a little new for the purpose."

Charles went rapidly ahead with his painting as he replied. "You are right. It seems likely that Orab made copies of the original record which he found, and placed the copies with his supplement on several high places around the globe. And it is possible that others after Orab, but long before our time, read the records and moved them for safekeeping. The copy that Junipero Serra found may have been here a mere twenty thousand years, or so."

CHAPTER NINE

FLEDGLINGS FLY

"WE COULD HANG AROUND HERE for fifty years, learning new things, but in the mean time we wouldn't be getting anywhere. I, for one, am ready to go back." Phil crushed out a cigaret and looked around at his two friends.

Coburn pursed his lips and slowly nodded his head. "I feel the same way, Phil. There is no limit to what we could learn here, of course, but there comes a time when you just have to use some of the things you learn, or it just boils up inside. I think we had better tell the Senior, and get about doing it."

Joan nodded vigorously. "Uh huh. I think so, too. There's work to be done, and the place to do it is Western U.—not up here in Never-Never land. Boy, I can hardly wait to see old Brinckley's face when we get through with him!"

Huxley sought out the mind of Ephraim Howe. The other two waited for him to confer, courteously refraining from attempting to enter the telepathic conversation. "He says he had been expecting to hear from us, and that he intends to make it a full conference. He'll meet us here."

"Full conference? Everybody on the mountain?"

"Everybody—on the mountain, or not. I gather it's customary when new members decide what their work will be."

"Whew!" exclaimed Joan, "that gives me stage fright just to think about it. Who's going to speak for us? It won't be little Joan."

"How about you, Ben?"

"Well . . . if you wish."

"Take over."

They meshed into rapport. As long as they remained so, Ben's voice would express the combined thought of the trio. Ephraim Howe entered alone, but they were aware that he was in rapport with, and spokesman for, not only the adepts on the mountainside, but also the two-hundred-odd full-geniuses scattered about the country.

The conference commenced with direct mind-to-mind exchange:

—"*We feel that it is time we were at work. We have not learned all that there is to learn, it is true; nevertheless, we need to use our present knowledge.*"

—"*That is well and entirely as it should be, Benjamin. You have learned all that we can teach you at this time. Now you must take what you have learned out into the world, and use it, in order that knowledge may mature into wisdom.*"

—"*Not only for that reason do we wish to leave, but for another more urgent. As you yourself have taught us, the crisis approaches. We want to fight it.*"

—"*How do you propose to fight the forces bringing on the crisis?*"

—"*Well . . .*" Ben did not use the word, but the delay in his thought produced the impression. "*As we see it, in order to make men free, free so that they may develop as men and not as animals; it is necessary that we undo what the Young Men did. The Young Men refused to permit any but their own select few to share in the racial heritage of ancient knowledge. For men again to become free and strong and independent it is necessary to return to each man his ancient knowledge and his ancient powers.*"

—"*That is true; what do you intend to do about it?*"

—"*We will go out and tell about it. We all three are in the educational system; we can make ourselves heard—I, in the medical school at Western; Phil and Joan in the department of psychology. With the training you have given us we can overturn the traditional ideas in short order. We can start a renaissance in education that will prepare the way for everyone to receive the wisdom that you, our elders, can offer them.*"

—"*Do you think that it will be as simple as that?*"

—"*Why not? Oh, we don't expect it to be simple. We know that we will run head on into some of the most cherished misconceptions of everyone, but we can use that very fact to help. It will be spectacular; we can get publicity through it that will call attention to our work. You have taught us enough that we can prove that we are right. For example—suppose we put on a public demonstration of levitation, and proved before thousands of people that human mind could do the things we know it can? Suppose we said that anyone could learn such things who first learned the techniques of telepathy? Why, in a year, or two, the whole nation could be taught telepathy, and be ready for the reading of the records, and all that that implies!"*

Howe's mind was silent for several long minutes—no message reached them. The three stirred uneasily under his thoughtful, sober gaze. Finally,

—*"If it were as simple as that, would we not have done it before?"*

It was the turn of the three to be silent. Howe continued kindly,—*"Speak up, my children. Do not be afraid. Tell us your thoughts freely. You will not offend us."*

The thought that Coburn sent in answer was hesitant—*"It is difficult . . . Many of you are very old, and we know that all of you are wise. Nevertheless, it seems to us, in our youth, that you have waited overly long in acting. We feel—we feel that you have allowed the pursuit of understanding to sap your will to action. From our standpoint, you have waited from year to year, perfecting an organization that will never be perfected, while the storm that overturns the world is gathering its force."*

The elders pondered before Ephraim Howe answered.—*"It may be that you are right, dearly beloved children, yet it does not seem so to us. We have not attempted to place the ancient knowledge in the hands of all men because few are ready for it. It is no more safe in childish minds than matches in childish hands.*

—*"And yet . . . you may be right. Mark Twain thought so, and was given permission to tell all that he had learned. He did so, writing so that anyone ready for the knowledge could understand. No one did. In desperation he set forth specifically how to become telepathic. Still no one took him seriously. The more seriously he spoke, the more his readers laughed. He died embittered.*

—*"We would not have you believe that we have done nothing. This republic, with its uncommon emphasis on personal freedom and human dignity, would not have endured as long as it has had we not helped. We chose Lincoln. Oliver Wendell Holmes was one of us. Walt Whitman was our beloved brother. In a thousand ways we have supplied help, when needed, to avert a setback toward slavery and darkness."*

The thought paused, then continued. —*"Yet each must act as he sees it. It is still your decision to do this?"*

Ben spoke aloud, in a steady voice, "It is!"

—*"So let it be! Do you remember the history of Salem?"*

—*"Salem? Where the witchcraft trials were held? . . . Do you mean to warn us that we may be persecuted as witches?"*

—*"No. There are no laws against witchcraft today, of course. It would be better if there were. We hold no monopoly on the power of knowledge; do not expect an easy victory. Beware of those who hold some portion of the ancient knowledge and use it to a base purpose— witches . . . black magicians!"*

The conference concluded and rapport loosed, Ephraim Howe shook hands solemnly all around and bade them good-bye.

"I envy you kids," he said, "going off like Jack the Giant Killer to tackle the whole educational system. You've got your work cut out for you. Do you remember what Mark Twain said? 'God made an idiot for practice, then he made a school board.' Still, I'd like to come along."

"Why don't you, sir?"

"Eh? No, 'twouldn't do. I don't really believe in your plan. F'r instance—it was frequently a temptation during the years I spent peddlin' hardware in the State of Maine to show people better ways of doing things. But I didn't do it; people are used to paring knives and ice cream freezers, and they won't thank you to show them how to get along without them, just by the power of the mind. Not all at

74

once, anyhow. They'd read you out of meetin'—and lynch you, too, most probably.

"Still, I'll be keeping an eye on you."

Joan reached up and kissed him good-bye. They left.

CHAPTER TEN

LION'S MOUTH

PHIL PICKED HIS LARGEST CLASS to make the demonstration which was to get the newspapers interested in them.

They had played safe to the extent of getting back to Los Angeles and started with the fall semester before giving anyone cause to suspect that they possessed powers out of ordinary. Joan had been bound over not to levitate, not to indulge in practical jokes involving control over inanimate objects, not to startle strangers with weird abilities of any sort. She had accepted the injunctions meekly, so meekly that Coburn claimed to be worried.

"It's not normal," he objected. "She can't grow up as fast as all that. Let me see your tongue, my dear."

"Pooh," she answered, displaying that member in a most undiagnostic manner, "Master Ling said I was further advanced along the Way than either one of you."

" 'The heathen Chinee is peculiar.' He was probably just encouraging you to grow up. Seriously, Phil, hadn't we better put her into a deep hypnosis and scoot her back up the mountain for diagnosis and readjustment?"

"Ben Coburn, you cast an eye in my direction and I'll bung it out!"

Phil built up to his key demonstration with care. His lectures were sufficiently innocuous that he could afford to have his head of department drop in without fear of reprimand or interference. But the combined effect was to prepare the students emotionally for what was to come. Carefully selected assignments for collateral reading heightened his chances.

"Hypnosis is a subject but vaguely understood," he began his lecture on the selected day, "and formerly classed with witchcraft, magic, and so forth, as a silly superstition. But t is a commonplace thing today and easily demonstrated. Consequently the most conservative psychologists must recognize its existence and try to observe its characteristics." He went on cheerfully uttering bromides and commonplaces, while he sized up the emotional attitude of the class.

When he felt that they were ready to accept the ordinary phenomena of hypnosis without surprise, he called Joan, who had attended for the purpose, up to the front of the room. She went easily into a state of light hypnosis. They ran quickly through the small change of hypnotic phenomena—catalepsy, compulsion, post-hypnotic suggestion—while he kept up a running chatter about the relation between the minds of the operator and the subject, the possibility of direct telepathic control, the Rhine experiments, and similar matters, orthodox in themselves, but close to the borderline of heterodox thought.

Then he offered to attempt to reach the mind of the subject telepathically.

Each student was invited to write something on a slip of paper. A volunteer floor committee collected the slips, and handed them to Huxley one at a time. He solemnly went through the hocus-pocus of glancing at each one, while Joan read them off as his eyes rested on them. She stumbled convincingly once or twice. —"Nice work, kid." —"Thanks, pal. Can't I pep it up a little?" —"None of your bright ideas. Just keep on as you are. They're eating out of our hands now."

By such easy stages he led them around to the idea that mind and will could exercise control over the body much more complete than that ordinarily encountered. He passed lightly over the tales of Hindu holy men who could lift themselves up into the air and even travel from place to place.

"We have an exceptional opportunity to put such tales to practical test," he told them. "The subject believes fully any statement made by the operator. I shall tell Miss Freeman that she is to exert her will power, and rise up off the floor. It is certain that she will believe that she can do it. Her will

77

will be in an optimum condition to carry out the order, if it can be done. Miss Freeman!"

"Yes, Mr. Huxley."

"Exert your will. Rise up in the air!"

Joan rose straight up into the air, some six feet—until her head nearly touched the high ceiling. —*"How'm doin', pal?"* —*"Swell, kid, you're wowin' 'em. Look at 'em stare!"*

At that moment Brinckley burst into the room, rage in his eyes.

"Mr. Huxley, you have broken your word to me, and disgraced this university!" It was some ten minutes after the fiasco ending the demonstration. Huxley faced the president in Brinckley's private office.

"I made you no promise. I have not disgraced the school," Phil answered with equal pugnacity.

"You have indulged in cheap tricks of fake magic to bring your department into disrepute."

"So I'm a faker, am I? You stiff-necked old fossil—explain this one!" Huxley levitated himself until he floated three feet above the rug.

"Explain what?" To Huxley's amazement Brinckley seemed unaware that anything unusual was going on. He continued to stare at the point where Phil's head had been. His manner showed nothing but a slight puzzlement and annoyance at Huxley's apparently irrelevant remark.

Was it possible that the doddering old fool was so completely self-deluded that he could not observe anything that ran counter to his own preconceptions even when it happened directly under his eyes? Phil reached out with his mind and attempted to see what went on inside Brinckley's head. He got one of the major surprises of his life. He expected to find the floundering mental processes of near senility; he found . . . cold calculation, keen ability, set in a matrix of pure evil that sickened him.

It was just a glimpse, then he was cast out with a wrench that numbed his brain. Brinckley had discovered his spying and thrown up his defences—the hard defences of a disciplined mind.

Phil dropped back to the floor, and left the room, without a word, nor a backward glance.

From THE WESTERN STUDENT, October 3rd:

PSYCH PROF FIRED FOR FRAUD

. . . students' accounts varied, but all agreed that it had been a fine show. Fullback 'Buzz' Arnold told your reporter, "I hated to see it happen; Prof Huxley is a nice guy and he certainly put on a clever skit with some good deadpan acting. I could see how it was done, of course—it was the same the Great Arturo used in his turn at the Orpheum last spring. But I can see Doctor Brinckley's viewpoint; you can't permit monkey shines at a serious center of learning."

President Brinckley gave the STUDENT the following official statement: "It is with real regret that I announce the termination of Mr. Huxley's association with the institution—for the good of the University. Mr. Huxley had been repeatedly warned as to where his steps were leading him. He is a young man of considerable ability. Let us devoutly hope that this experience will serve as a lesson to him in whatever line of endeavor . . ."

Coburn handed the paper back to Huxley. "You know what happened to me?" he inquired.

"Something new?"

"Invited to resign . . . No publicity—just a gentle hint. My patients got well too fast; I'd quit using surgery, you know."

"How perfectly stinking!" This from Joan.

"Well," Ben considered, "I don't blame the medical director; Brinckley forced his hand. I guess we underrated the old cuss."

"Rather! Ben, he's every bit as capable as any one of us, and as for his motives—I gag when I think about it."

"And I thought he was just a were-mouse," grieved Joan. "We should have pushed him into the tar pits last spring. I told you to. What do we do now?"

"Go right ahead." Phil's reply was grim. "We'll turn the situation to our own advantage; we've gotten some publicity—we'll use it."

"What's the gag?"

"Levitation again. It's the most spectacular thing we've got for a crowd. Call in the papers, and tell 'em that we will publicly demonstrate levitation at noon tomorrow in Pershing Square."

"Won't the papers fight shy of sticking their necks out on anything that sounds as fishy as that?"

"Probably they would, but here's how we'll handle that: Make the whole thing just a touch screwball and give 'em plenty of funny angles to write up. Then they can treat it as a feature rather than as straight news. The lid's off, Joan—you can do anything you like; the screwier the better. Let's get going, troops—I'll call the News Service. Ben, you and Joan split the dailies between you."

The reporters were interested, certainly. They were interested in Joan's obvious good looks, cynically amused by Phil's flowing tie and bombastic claims, and seriously impressed by his taste in whiskey. They began to take notice when Coburn courteously poured drinks for them without bothering to touch the bottle.

But when Joan floated around the room while Phil rode a non-existent bicycle across the ceiling, they balked. "Honest, doc," as one of them put it, "we've got to eat—you don't expect us to go back and tell a city editor anything like this. Come clean; is it the whiskey, or just plain hypnotism?"

"Put it any way you like, gentlemen. Just be sure that you say that we will do it all over again in Pershing Square at noon tomorrow."

Phil's diatribe against Brinckley came as an anticlimax to the demonstration, but the reporters obligingly noted it.

Joan got ready for bed that night with a feeling of vague depression. The exhilaration of entertaining the newspaper boys had worn off. Ben had proposed supper and dancing to mark their last night of private life, but it had not been a success. To start with, they had blown a tire while coming down a steep curve on Beachwood Drive, and Phil's gray sedan had rolled over and over. They would have all been seriously injured had it not been for the automatic body control which they possessed.

When Phil examined the wreck, he expressed puzzlement as to its cause. "Those tires were perfectly all right," he maintained. "I had examined them all the way through this morning." But he insisted on continuing with their evening of relaxation.

The floor show seemed dull, the jokes crude and callous, after the light, sensitive humor they had learned to enjoy through association with Master Ling. The ponies in the chorus were young and beautiful—Joan had enjoyed watching them, but she made the mistake of reaching out to touch their minds. The incongruity of the vapid, insensitive spirits she found—in almost every instance—added to her malaise.

She was relieved when the floor show ended and Ben asked her to dance. Both of the men were good dancers, especially Coburn, and she fitted herself into his arms contentedly. Her pleasure didn't last; a drunken couple bumped into them repeatedly. The man was quarrelsome, the woman shrilly vitriolic. Joan asked her escorts to take her home.

These things bothered her as she prepared for bed. Joan, who had never known acute physical fear in her life, feared just one thing—the corrosive, dirty emotions of the poor in spirit. Malice, envy, spite, the snide insults of twisted, petty minds; these things could hurt her, just by being in her

81

presence, even if she were not the direct object of the attack. She was not yet sufficiently mature to have acquired a smooth armor of indifference to the opinions of the unworthy.

After a summer in the company of men of good will, the incident with the drunken couple dismayed her. She felt dirtied by the contact. Worse still, she felt an outlander, a stranger in a strange land.

She awakened sometime in the night with the sense of loneliness increased to overwhelming proportions. She was acutely aware of the three-million-odd living beings around her, but the whole city seemed alive only with malignant entities, jealous of her, anxious to drag her down to their own ignoble status. This attack on her spirit, this attempt to despoil the sanctity of her inner being, assumed an almost corporate nature. It seemed to her that it was nibbling at the edges of her mind, snuffling at her defences.

Terrified, she called out to Ben and Phil. There was no answer; her mind could not find them.

The filthy thing that threatened her was aware of her failure; she could feel it leer. In open panic she called to the Senior.

No answer. This time the thing spoke—"That way, too, is closed."

As hysteria claimed her, as her last defences crumbled, she was caught in the arms of a stronger spirit, whose calm, untroubled goodness encysted her against the evil thing that stalked her.

"Ling!" she cried, "Master Ling!" before racking sobs claimed her.

She felt the quiet, reassuring humor of his smile while the fingers of his mind reached out and smoothed away the tensions of her fear. Presently she slept.

His mind stayed with her all through the night, and talked with her, until she awakened.

Ben and Phil listened to her account of the previous night

with worried faces. "That settles it," Phil decided. "We've been too careless. From now on until this thing is finished, we stay in rapport day and night, awake and asleep. As a matter of fact, I had a bad time of it myself last night, though nothing equal to what happened to Joan."

"So did I, Phil. What happened to you?"

"Nothing very much—just a long series of nightmares in which I kept losing confidence in my ability to do any of the things we learned on Shasta. What about you?"

"Same sort of thing, with variations. I operated all night long, and all of my patients died on the table. Not very pleasant—but something else happened that wasn't a dream. You know I still use an old-fashioned straight-razor; I was shaving away, paying no attention to it, when it jumped in my hand and cut a big gash in my throat. See? It's not entirely healed yet." He indicated a thin red line which ran diagonally down the right side of his neck.

"Why, Ben!" squealed Joan, "you might have been killed."

"That's what I thought," he agreed dryly.

"You know, kids," Phil said slowly, "these things aren't accidental—"

"Open up in there!" The order was bawled from the other side of the door. As one mind, their senses of direct perception jumped through solid oak and examined the speaker. Plain-clothes did not conceal the profession of the over-size individual waiting there, even had they not been able to see the gold shield on his vest. A somewhat smaller, but equally officious, man waited with him.

Ben opened the door and inquired gently, "What do you want?"

The larger man attempted to come in. Coburn did not move.

"I asked you your business."

"Smart guy, eh? I'm from police headquarters. You Huxley?"

"No."

"Coburn?" Ben nodded.

"You'll do. That Huxley behind you? Don't either of you ever stay home? Been here all night?"

"No," said Coburn frostily, "not that it is any of your business."

"I'll decide about that. I want to talk to you two. I'm from the bunco squad. What's this game you were giving the boys yesterday?"

"No game, as you call it. Come down to Pershing Square at noon today, and see for yourself."

"You won't be doing anything in Pershing Square today, Bud."

"Why not?"

"Park Commission's orders."

"What authority?"

"Huh?"

"By what act, or ordinance, do they deny the right of private citizens to make peaceful use of a public place? Who is that with you?"

The smaller man identified himself. "Name's Ferguson, D.A.'s office. I want your pal Huxley on a criminal libel complaint. I want you two's witnesses."

Ben's stare became colder, if possible. "Do either of you," he inquired, in gently snubbing tones, "have a warrant?"

They looked at each other and failed to reply. Ben continued, "Then it is hardly profitable to continue this conversation, is it?" and closed the door in their faces.

He turned around to his companions and grinned. "Well, they are closing in. Let's see what the papers gave us."

They found just one story. It said nothing about their proposed demonstration, but related that Doctor Brinckley had sworn a complaint charging Phil with criminal libel. "That's the first time I ever heard of four metropolitan papers refusing a juicy news story," was Ben's comment, "what are you going to do about Brinckley's charge?"

"Nothing," Phil told him, "except possibly libel him again. If he goes through with it, it will be a beautiful opportunity to prove our claims in court. Which reminds me—we don't want our plans interfered with today; those bird dogs may be back with warrants most any time. Where'll we hide out?"

On Ben's suggestion they spent the morning buried in the downtown public library. At five minutes to twelve, they flagged a taxi, and rode to Pershing Square.

They stepped out of the cab into the arms of six sturdy policemen.

—*"Ben, Phil, how much longer do I have to put up with this?"*

—*"Steady, kid. Don't get upset."*

—*"I'm not, but why should we stay pinched when we can duck out anytime?"*

—*"That's the point; we can escape anytime. We've never been arrested before; let's see what it's like."*

They were gathered that night late around the fireplace in Joan's house. Escape had presented no difficulties, but they had waited until an hour when the jail was quiet to prove that stone walls do not a prison make for a person adept in the powers of the mind.

Ben was speaking, "I'd say we had enough data to draw a curve now."

"Which is?"

"You state it."

"All right. We came down from Shasta thinking that all we had to overcome was stupidity, ignorance, and a normal amount of human contrariness and cussedness. Now we know better. Any attempt to place the essentials of the ancient knowledge in the hands of the common people is met by a determined, organized effort to prevent it, and to destroy, or disable the one who tries it."

"It's worse than that," amended Ben, "I spent our rest in the clink looking over the city. I wondered why the district attorney should take such an interest in us, so I took a look into his mind. I found out who his boss was, and took a look at *his* mind. What I found there interested me so much that I had to run up to the state capital and see what made things tick there. That took me back to Spring Street and the financial district. Believe it or not, from there I had to look up some of the most sacred cows in the community—clergymen, clubwomen, business leaders, and stuff." He paused.

"Well, what about it? Don't tell me everybody is out of step but Willie—I'll break down and cry."

"No—that was the odd part about it. Nearly all of these heavyweights were good Joes, people you'd like to know. But usually—not always, but usually—the good Joes were dominated by someone they trusted, someone who had helped them to get where they were, and these dominants were not good Joes, to state it gently. I couldn't get into all of their minds, but where I was able to get in, I found the same sort of thing that Phil found in Brinckley—cold calculated awareness that their power lay in keeping the people in ignorance."

Joan shivered. "That's a sweet picture you paint, Ben—just the right thing for a bed-time story. What's our next move?"

"What do you suggest?"

"Me? I haven't reached any conclusion. Maybe we should take on these tough babies one at a time, and smear 'em."

"How about you, Phil?"

"I haven't anything better to offer. We'll have to plan a shrewd campaign, however."

"Well, I do have something to suggest myself."

"Let's have it."

"Admit that we blindly took on more than we could handle. Go back to Shasta and ask for help."

"Why, Ben!" Joan's dismay was matched by Phil's unhappy face. Ben went on stubbornly, "Sure, I know it's gravelling, but pride is too expensive and the job is too—"

He broke off when he noticed Joan's expression. "What is it kid?"

"We'll have to make some decision quickly—that is a police car that just stopped out in front."

Ben turned back to Phil. "What'll it be; stay and fight, or go back for re-inforcements?"

"Oh, you're right. I've known it ever since I got a look at Brinckley's mind—but I hated to admit it."

The three stepped out into the patio, joined hands, and shot straight up into the air.

CHAPTER ELEVEN

"A LITTLE CHILD SHALL LEAD THEM."

"WELCOME HOME!" Ephraim Howe met them when they landed. "Glad to have you back." He led them into his own private apartment. "Rest yourselves while I stir up the fire a mite." He chucked a wedge of pinewood into the wide grate, pulled his homely old rocking chair around so that it faced both the fire and his guests, and settled down. "Now suppose you tell me all about it. No, I'm not hooked in with the others—you can make a full report to the council when you're ready."

"As a matter of fact, don't you already know everything that happened to us, Mr. Howe?" Phil looked directly at the Senior as he spoke.

"No, I truly don't. We let you go at it your own way, with Ling keeping an eye out to see that you didn't get hurt. He has made no report to me."

"Very well, sir." They took turns telling him all that had happened to them, occasionally letting him see directly through their minds the events they had taken part in.

When they were through Howe gave them his quizzical smile and inquired, "So you've come around to the viewpoint of the council?"

"No, sir!" It was Phil who answered him. "We are more convinced of the need for positive, immediate action than we were when we left—but we are convinced, too, that we aren't strong enough nor wise enough to handle it alone. We've come back to ask for help, and to urge the council to abandon its policy of teaching only those who show that they are ready, and, instead, to reach out and teach as many minds as can accept your teachings.

"You see, sir, our antagonists don't wait. They are active

all the time. They've won in Asia, they are in the ascendancy in Europe, they may win here in America, while we wait for an opportunity."

"Have you any method to suggest for tackling the problem?"

"No, that's why we came back. When we tried to teach others what we knew, we were stopped."

"That's the rub," Howe agreed. "I've been pretty much of your opinion for a good many years, but it is hard to do. What we have to give can't be printed in a book, nor broadcast over the air. It must be passed directly from mind to mind, wherever we find a mind ready to receive it."

They finished the discussion without finding a solution. Howe told them not to worry. "Go along," he said, "and spend a few weeks in meditation and rapport. When you get an idea that looks as if it might work, bring it in and we'll call the council together to consider it."

"But, Senior," Joan protested for the trio, "you see—Well, we had hoped to have the advice of the council in working out a plan. We don't know where to start, else we wouldn't have come back."

He shook his head. "You are the newest of the brethren, the youngest, the least experienced. Those are your virtues, not your disabilities. The very fact that you have not spent years of this life in thinking in terms of eons and races gives you an advantage. Too broad a viewpoint, too philosophical an outlook paralyzes the will. I want you three to consider it alone."

They did as he asked. For weeks they discussed it in rapport as a single mind, hammered at it in spoken conversation, meditated its ramifications. They roamed the nation with their minds, examining the human spirits that lay behind political and social action. With the aid of the archives they learned the techniques by which the brotherhood of adepts had interceded in the past when freedom of thought and action in America had been threatened. They proposed and rejected dozens of schemes.

"We should go into politics," Phil told the other two, "as our brothers did in the past. If we had a Secretary of Education, appointed from among the elders, he could found a national academy in which freedom of thought would really prevail, and it could be the source from which the ancient knowledge could spread."

Joan put in an objection.

"Suppose you lose the election?"

"Huh?"

"Even with all the special powers that the adepts have, it 'ud be quite a chore to line up delegates for a national convention to get our candidate nominated, then get him elected in the face of all the political machines, pressure groups, newspapers, favorite sons, et cetera, et cetera, et cetera.

"And remember this, the opposition can fight as dirty as it pleases, but we have to fight fair, or we defeat our own aims."

Ben nodded. "I am afraid she is right, Phil. But you are absolutely right in one thing; this is a problem of education." He stopped to meditate, his mind turned inward.

Presently he resumed. "I wonder if we have been tackling this job from the right end? We've been thinking of reeducating adults, already set in their ways. How about the children? They haven't crystallized; wouldn't they be easier to teach?"

Joan sat up, her eyes bright. "Ben, you've got it!"

Phil shook his head doggedly. "No. I hate to throw cold water, but there is no way to go about it. Children are constantly in the care of adults; we couldn't get to them. Don't think for a moment that you could get past local school boards; they are the tightest little oligarchies in the whole political system."

They were sitting in a group of pine trees on the lower slopes of Mount Shasta. A little group of human figures came into view below them and climbed steadily toward the spot where the three rested. The discussion was suspended until the group moved beyond earshot. The trio watched them with casual, friendly interest.

They were all boys, ten to fifteen years old, except the leader, who bore his sixteen years with the serious dignity befitting one who is responsible for the safety and wellbeing of younger charges. They were dressed in khaki shorts and shirts, campaign hats, neckerchiefs embroidered with a conifer and the insignia ALPINE PATROL, TROOP I, Each carried a staff and a knapsack.

As the procession came abreast of the adults, the patrol leader gave them a wave in greeting, the merit badges on his sleeve flashing in the sun. The three waved back and watched them trudge out of sight up the slope.

Phil watched them with a faraway look. "Those were the good old days," he said; "I almost envy them."

"Were you one?" Ben said, his eyes still on the boys. "I remember how proud I was the day I got my merit badge in first aid."

"Born to be a doctor, eh, Ben?" commented Joan, her eyes maternal, approving. "I didn't—say!"

"What's up?"

"Phil! That's your answer! That's how to reach the children in spite of parents and school boards."

She snapped into telepathic contact, her ideas spilling excitedly into their minds. They went into rapport and ironed out the details. After a time Ben nodded and spoke aloud.

"It might work," he said, "let's go back and talk it over with Ephraim."

"Senator Moulton, these are the young people I was telling you about." Almost in awe, Joan looked at the face of the little white-haired, old man whose name had become a synonym for integrity. She felt the same impulse to fold her hands across her middle and bow which Master Ling inspired. She noted that Ben and Phil were having trouble not to seem gawky and coltish.

Ephraim Howe continued, "I have gone into their scheme and I think it is practical. If you do too, the council will go ahead with it. But it largely depends on you."

The Senator took them to himself with a smile, the smile that had softened the hearts of two generations of hard politicians. "Tell me about it," he invited.

They did so—how they had tried and failed at Western University, how they had cudgeled their brains for a way, how a party of boys on a hike up the mountain had given them an inspiration. "You see, Senator, if we could just get enough boys up here all at once, boys too young to have been corrupted by their environment, and already trained, as these boys are, in the ideals of the ancients,—human dignity, helpfulness, self-reliance, kindness, all those things set forth in their code—if we could get even five thousand such boys up here all at once, we could train them in telepathy, and how to impart telepathy to others.

"Once they were taught, and sent back to their homes, each one would be a center for spreading the knowledge. The antagonists could never stop it; it would be too wide spread, epidemic. In a few years every child in the country would' be telepathic, and they would even teach their elders—those that haven't grown too calloused to learn.

"And once a human being is telepathic, we can lead him along the path of the ancient wisdom!"

Moulton was nodding, and talking to himself. "Yes. Yes indeed. It could be done. Fortunately Shasta is a national park. Let me see, who is on that committee? It would take a joint resolution and a small appropriation. Ephraim, old friend, I am afraid I shall have to practice a little logrolling to accomplish this, will you forgive me?"

Howe grinned broadly.

"Oh, I mean it," Moulton continued, "people are so cynical, so harsh, about political expediency—even some of our brothers. Let me see, this will take about two years, I think, before the first camp can be held—"

"As long as that?" Joan was disappointed.

"Oh, yes, my dear. There are two bills to get before Congress, and much arranging to do to get them passed in the face of a full legislative calendar. There are arrangements to be made with the railroads and bus companies to give the boys special rates so that they can afford to come. We must start a publicity campaign to make the idea popular. Then there must be time for as many of our brothers as possible to get into the administration of the movement in order that the camp executives may be liberally interspersed with adepts. Fortunately I am a national trustee of the organization. Yes, I can manage it in two years' time, I believe."

"Good heavens!" protested Phil; "why wouldn't it be more to the point to teleport them here, teach them, and teleport them back?"

"You do not know what you are saying, my son. Can we abolish force by using it? Every step must be voluntary, accomplished by reason and persuasion. Each human being must free himself; freedom cannot be thrust on him. Besides, is two years long to wait to accomplish a job that has been waiting since the Deluge?"

"I'm sorry, sir."

"Do not be. Your youthful impatience has made it possible to do the job at all."

CHAPTER TWELVE

"YE SHALL KNOW THE TRUTH—"

ON THE LOWER SLOPES of Mount Shasta, down near McCloud, the camp grew up. When the last of the spring snow was still hiding in the deeper gullies and on the north sides of ridges, U.S. Army Quartermaster trucks came lumbering over a road built the previous fall by the army engineers. Pyramid tents were broken out and were staked down in rows on the bosom of a gently rolling alp. Cook shacks, an infirmary, a headquarters building took shape. Camp Mark Twain was changing from blueprint to actuality.

Senator Moulton, his toga laid aside for breeches, leggings, khaki shirt, and a hat marked CAMP DIRECTOR, puttered around the field, encouraging, making decisions for the straw bosses, and searching, ever searching the minds of all who came into or near the camp for any purpose. Did anyone suspect? Had anyone slipped in who might be associated with partial adepts who opposed the real purpose of the camp? Too late to let anything slip now—too late, and too much at stake.

In the middle west, in the deep south, in New York City and New England, in the mountains and on the coast, boys were packing suitcases, buying special Shasta Camp round-trip tickets, talking about it with their envious contemporaries.

And all over the country the antagonists of human liberty, of human dignity—the racketeers, the crooked political figures, the shysters, the dealers in phony religions, the sweatshoppers, the petty authoritarians, all of the key figures among the traffickers in human misery and human oppression, themselves somewhat adept in the arts of the mind and acutely aware of the danger of free knowledge—all of this unholy breed stirred uneasily and wondered what was taking place. Moulton had never been associated with anything but ill for them; Mount Shasta was one place they had never been able to touch—they hated the very name of the place. They recalled old stories, and shivered.

They shivered, but they acted.

Special transcontinental buses loaded with the chosen boys—could the driver be corrupted? Could his mind be taken over? Could tires, or engine, be tampered with? Trains were taken over by the youngsters. Could a switch be thrown? Could the drinking water be polluted?

Other eyes watched. A trainload of boys moved westward; in it, or flying over it, his direct perception blanketing the surrounding territory, and checking the motives of every mind within miles of his charges, was stationed at least one adept whose single duty it was to see that those boys reached Shasta safely.

Probably some of the boys would never have reached there had not the opponents of human freedom been caught off balance, doubtful, unorganized. For vice has this defect; it cannot be truly intelligent. Its very motives are its weakness. The attempts made to prevent the boys reaching Shasta were scattered and abortive. The adepts had taken the offensive for once, and their moves were faster and more rationally conceived than their antagonists'.

Once in camp a tight screen surrounded the whole of Mount Shasta National Park. The Senior detailed adepts to point patrol night and day to watch with every sense at their command for mean or malignant spirits. The camp itself was purged. Two of the councilors, and some twenty of the boys, were sent home when examination showed them to be damaged souls. The boys were not informed of their deformity, but plausible excuses were found for the necessary action.

The camp resembled superficially a thousand other such camps. The courses in woodcraft were the same. The courts of honor met as usual to examine candidates. There were the usual sings around the campfire in the evening, the same setting-up exercises before breakfast. The slightly greater emphasis on the oath and the law of the organization was not noticeable.

Each one of the boys made at least one overnight hike in the course of the camp. In groups of fifteen or twenty they would set out in the morning in company of a councilor. That each councilor supervising such hikes was an adept was not evident, but it so happened. Each boy carried his blanket roll, and knapsack of rations, his canteen, knife, compass, and hand axe.

They camped that night on the bank of a mountain stream, fed by the glaciers, whose rush sounded in their ears as they ate supper.

Phil started out with such a group one morning during the first week of the camp. He worked around the mountain to the east in order to keep well away from the usual tourist haunts.

After supper they sat around the campfire. Phil told them stories of the holy men of the east and their reputed powers, and of Saint Francis and the birds. He was in the middle of one of his yarns when a figure appeared within the circle of firelight.

Or rather figures. They saw an old man, in clothes that Davy Crockett might have worn, flanked by two beasts, on his left side a mountain lion, who purred when he saw the fire, on his right a buck of three points, whose soft brown eyes stared calmly into theirs.

Some of the boys were alarmed at first, but Phil told them quietly to widen their circle and make room for the strangers. They sat in decent silence for a while, the boys getting used to the presence of the animals. In time one of the boys timidly stroked the big cat, who responded by rolling over and presenting his soft belly. The boy looked up at the old man and asked,

"What is his name, Mister—"

"Ephraim. His name is Freedom."

"My, but he's tame! How do you get him to be so tame?"

"He reads my thoughts and trusts me. Most things are friendly when they know you—and most people."

The boy puzzled for a moment. "How can he read your thoughts?"

"It's simple. You can read his, too. Would you like to learn how?"

"Jiminy!"

"Just look into my eyes for a moment. There! Now look into his."

"Why—Why—I really believe I can!"

—*"Of course you can. And mine, too. I'm not talking out loud. Had you noticed?"*

—*"Why, so you're not. I'm reading your thoughts!"*

—*"And I'm reading yours. Easy, isn't it?"*

With Phil's help Howe had them all conversing by thought transference inside an hour. Then to calm them down he told them stories for another hour, stories that constituted an important part of their curriculum. He helped Phil get them to sleep, then left, the animals following after him.

The next morning Phil was confronted at once by a young sceptic. "Say, did I dream all that about an old man and a puma and a deer?"

—*"Did you?"*

—*"You're doing it now!"*

—*"Certainly I am. And so are you. Now go tell the other boys the same thing."*

Before they got back to camp, he advised them not to speak about it to any other of the boys who had not as yet had their overnight hike, but that they test their new powers by trying it on any boy who had had his first all-night hike.

All was well until one of the boys had to return home in answer to a message that his father was ill. The elders would not wipe his mind clean of his new knowledge; instead they kept careful track of him. In time he talked, and the word reached the antagonists almost at once. Howe ordered the precautions of the telepathic patrol redoubled.

97

The patrol was able to keep out malicious persons, but i was not numerous enough to keep everything out. Forest fire broke out on the windward side of the camp late one night No human being had been close to the spot; telekinetics wa the evident method.

But what control over matter from a distance can do, i can also undo. Moulton squeezed the flame out with his will refused it permission to burn, bade its vibrations to stop.

For the time being the enemy appeared to cease attempt to do the boys physical harm. But the enemy had not give up. Phil received a frantic call from one of the younger boy to come at once to the tent the boy lived in; his patrol leade was very sick. Phil found the lad in a state of hysteria, and being restrained from doing himself an injury by the othe boys in the tent. He had tried to cut his throat with his jack knife and had gone berserk when one of the other boys had grabbed his hand.

Phil took in the situation quickly and put in a call to Ben
—"Ben! Come at once. I need you."

Ben did so, zipping through the air and flying in throug the door of the tent almost before Phil had time to lay the boy on his cot and start forcing him into a trance. The lad' startled tent mates did not have time to decide that Dr. Be had been flying before he was standing in a normal fashion alongside their councilor.

Ben greeted him with tight communication, shutting th boys out of the circuit. —"What's up?"
—"They've gotten to him . . . and damn near wrecked him."
—"How?"
—"Preyed on his mind. Tried to make him suicide. But I trance back the hookup. Who do you think tried to do him in?—Brinckley!
—"No!"
—"Definitely. You take over here; I'm going after Brinckley. Tel the Senior to have a watch put on all the boys who have been traine to be sensitive to telepathy. I'm afraid that any of them may be gotte

98

at before we can teach them how to defend themselves." With that he was gone, leaving the boys half convinced of levitation.

He had not gone very far, was still gathering speed, when he heard a welcome voice in his head.

—*"Phil! Phil! Wait for me."*

He slowed down for a few seconds. A smaller figure flashed alongside his and grasped his hand. "It's a good thing I stay hooked in with you two. You'd have gone off to tackle that dirty old so-and-so without me."

He tried to maintain his dignity. "If I had thought that you should be along on this job, I'd have called you, Joan."

"Nonsense! And also fiddlesticks! You might get hurt, tackling him all alone. Besides, I'm going to push him into the tar pits."

He sighed and gave up. "Joan, my dear, you are a bloodthirsty wench with ten thousand incarnations to go before you reach beatitude."

"I don't want to reach beatitude; I want to do old Brinckley in."

"Come along, then. Let's make some speed."

They were south of the Tehachapi by now and rapidly approaching Los Angeles. They flitted over the Sierra Madre range, shot across San Fernando Valley, clipped the top of Mount Hollywood, and landed on the lawn of the President's Residence at Western University. Brinckley saw, or felt, them coming and tried to run for it, but Phil grappled with him.

He shot one thought to Joan. —*"You stay out of this, kid, unless I yell for help."*

Brinckley did not give up easily. His mind reached out and tried to engulf Phil's. Huxley felt himself slipping, giving way before the evil onslaught. It seemed as though he were being dragged down, drowned, in filthy quicksand.

But he steadied himself and fought back.

When Phil had finished that which was immediately necessary with Brinckley, he stood up and wiped his hands, as if to cleanse himself of the spiritual slime he had embraced. "Let's get going," he said to Joan, "we're pushed for time."

"What did you do to him, Phil?" She stared with fascinated disgust at the thing on the ground.

"Little enough. I placed him in stasis. I've got to save him for use—for a time. Up you go, girl. Out of here—before we're noticed."

Up they shot, with Brinckley's body swept along behind by tight telekinetic bond. They stopped above the clouds. Brinckley floated beside them, starfished, eyes popping, mouth loose, his smooth pink face expressionless. —*"Ben!"* Huxley was sending, *"Ephraim Howe! Ambrose! To me! To me! Hurry!"*

—*"Coming, Phil!"* came Coburn's answer.

—*"I hear."* The strong calm thought held the quality of the Senior. *"What is it, son? Tell me."*

—*"Not time!"* snapped Phil. *"Yourself, Senior, and all others that can. Rendezvous! Hurry!"*

—*"We come."* The thought was still calm, unhurried. But there were two ragged holes in the roof of Moulton's tent. Moulton and Howe were already out of sight of Camp Mark Twain.

Slashing, slicing through the air they came, the handful of adepts who guarded the fire. From five hundred miles to the north they came, racing pigeons hurrying home. Camp councilors, two-thirds of the small group of camp matrons, some few from scattered points on the continent, they came in response to Huxley's call for help and the Senior's unprecedented tocsin. A housewife turned out the fire in the oven and disappeared into the sky. A taxi driver stopped his car and left his fares without a word. Research groups on Shasta broke their tight rapport, abandoned their beloved work, and came—fast!

"And now, Philip?" Howe spoke orally as he arrested his trajectory and hung beside Huxley.

Huxley flung a hand toward Brinckley. "He has what we need to know to strike now! Where's Master Ling?"

"He and Mrs. Draper guard the Camp."

"I need him. Can she do it alone?"

Clear and mellow, her voice rang in his head from half a state away. —"*I can!*"

—"*The tortoise flies.*" The second thought held the quality of deathless merriment which was the unmistakable characteristic of the ancient Chinese.

Joan felt a soft touch at her mind, then Master Ling was among them, seated carefully tailor-fashion on nothingness. "I attend; my body follows," he announced. "Can we not proceed?"

Whereupon Joan realized that he had borrowed the faculties of her mind to project himself into their presence more quickly than he could levitate the distance. She felt unreasonably flattered by the attention.

Huxley commenced at once. "Through *his* mind—" He indicated Brinckley, "I have learned of many others with whom there can be no truce. We must search them out, deal with them at once, before they can rally from what has happened to him. But I need help. Master, will you extend the present and examine him?"

Ling had tutored them in discrimination of time and perception of the present, taught them to stand off and perceive duration from eternity. But he was incredibly more able than his pupils. He could split the beat of a fly's wing into a thousand discrete instants, or grasp a millennium as a single flash of experience. His discrimination of time and space was bound neither by his metabolic rate nor by his molar dimensions.

Now he poked gingerly at Brinckley's brain like one who seeks a lost jewel in garbage. He felt out the man's memory patterns and viewed his life as one picture. Joan, with amazement, saw his everpresent smile give way to a frown of distaste. His mind had been left open to any who cared to watch. He peered through his mind, then cut off. If there were that many truly vicious spirits in the world, she preferred to

encounter them one at a time, as necessary, not experien
them all at once.

Master Ling's body joined the group, melted into his pr
jection.

Huxley, Howe, Moulton, and Bierce followed the Chinese
delicate work with close attention. Howe's face was bleak
impassive; Moulton's face, aged to androgynous sensitivit
moved from side to side while he clucked disapproval of suc
wickedness. Bierce looked more like Mark Twain than eve
Twain in an implacable, lowering rage.

Master Ling looked up. "Yes, yes," said Moulton, "I su
pose we must act, Ephraim."

"We have no choice," Huxley stated, with a complete
unconscious disregard of precedent. "Will you assign tl
tasks, Senior?"

Howe glanced sharply at him. "No, Philip. No. Go ahea
Carry on."

Huxley checked himself in surprise for the briefest instan
then took his cue. "You'll help me, Master Ling. Ben!"

"Waiting!"

He meshed mind to mind, had Ling show him his oppo
nent and the data he needed. —*"Got it? Need any help?"*

—*"Grandfather Stonebender is enough."*

—*"Okay. Nip off and attend to it."*

—*"Chalk it up."* He was gone, a rush of air in his wake.

—*"This one is yours, Senator Moulton."*

—*"I know."* And Moulton was gone.

By ones and twos he gave them their assignments, and c
they went to do that which must be done. There was r
argument. Many of them had been aware long before Huxle
was that a day of action must inevitably come to pass, bi
they had waited with quiet serenity, busy with the work i
hand, till time should incubate the seed.

In a windowless study of a mansion on Long Island, soun
proofed, cleverly locked and guarded, ornately furnished,
group of five was met—three men, one woman, and a thi

1 a wheel chair. It glared at the other four in black fury,
lared without eyes, for its forehead dropped unbroken to its
heekbones, a smooth sallow expanse.

A lap robe, tucked loosely across the chair masked, but
id not hide, the fact that the creature had no legs.

It gripped the arms of the chair. "Must I do *all* the think-
g for you fools?" it asked in a sweet gentle voice. "You,
rthurson—you let Moulton slip that Shasta Bill past the
enate. Moron." The epithet was uttered caressingly.

Arthurson shifted in his chair. "I examined his mind. The
ill was harmless. It was a swap on the Missouri Valley deal.
told you."

"You examined his mind, eh? Hmm—he led you on a
ersonally conducted tour, you fool. A *Shasta* bill! When will
ou mindless idiots learn that no good ever came out of
hasta?" It smiled approvingly.

"Well, how was I to know? I thought a camp near the
nountain might confuse . . . *them*."

"Mindless idiot. The time will come when I will find you
ispensable." The thing did not wait for the threat to sink
n, but continued, "Enough of that now. We must move
) repair the damage. *They* are on the offensive now.
gnes—"

"Yes." The woman answered.

"Your preaching has got to pick up—"

"I've done my best."

"Not good enough. I've got to have a wave of religious
ysteria that will wash out the Bill of Rights—*before* the
hasta camp breaks up for the summer. We will have to act
st before that time and we can't be hampered by a lot of
galisms."

"It can't be done."

"Shut up. It can be done. Your temple will receive endow-
nents this week which you are to use for countrywide tele-
sion hookups. At the proper time you will discover a new
nessiah."

"Who?"

103

"Brother Artemis."

"*That* cornbelt pipsqueak? Where do I come in on this?"

"You'll get yours. But you can't head this movement; th
country won't take a woman in the top spot. The two of yo
will lead a march on Washington and take over. The Son
of '76 will fill out your ranks and do the street fighting
Weems, that's your job."

The man addressed demurred. "It will take three, mayb
four months to indoctrinate them."

"You have three weeks. It would be well not to fail."

The last of the three men broke his silence. "What's th
hurry, Chief? Seems to me that you are getting yourself i
a panic over a few kids."

"I'll be the judge. Now you are to time an epidemic o
strikes to tie the country up tight at the time of the march o
Washington."

"I'll need some incidents."

"You'll get them. You worry about the unions; I'll tak
care of the Merchants' and Commerce League myself. Yo
give me one small strike tomorrow. Get your pickets out an
I will have four or five of them shot. The publicity will b
ready. Agnes, you preach a sermon about it."

"Slanted which way?"

It rolled its non-existent eyes up to the ceiling. "Must
think of everything? It's elementary. Use your minds."

The last man to speak laid down his cigar carefully an
said, "What's the real rush, Chief?"

"I've told you."

"No, you haven't. You've kept your mind closed an
haven't let us read your thoughts once. You've known abou
the Shasta camp for months. Why this sudden excitemen
You aren't slipping, are you? Come on, spill it. You can
expect us to follow if you are slipping."

The eyeless one looked him over carefully. "Hanson," h
said, in still sweeter tones, "you have been feeling your siz
for months. Would you care to match your strength wit
mine?"

The other looked at his cigar. "I don't mind if I do."

"You will. But not tonight. I haven't time to select and train new lieutenants. Therefore I will tell you what the urgency is. I can't raise Brinckley. He's fallen out of communication. There is not *time*—"

"You are correct," said a new voice. "There is not time."

The five jerked puppetlike to face its source. Standing side by side in the study were Ephraim Howe and Joan Freeman.

Howe looked at the thing. "I've waited for this meeting," he said cheerfully, "and I've saved you for myself."

The creature got out of its wheelchair and moved through the air at Howe. Its height and position gave an unpleasant sensation that it walked on invisible legs. Howe signalled to Joan—"*It starts. Can you hold the others, my dear?*"

—"*I think so.*"

—"*Now!*" Howe brought to bear everything he had learned in one hundred and thirty busy years, concentrated on the single problem of telekinetic control. He avoided, refused contact with the mind of the evil thing before him and turned his attention to destroying its physical envelope.

The thing stopped.

Slowly, slowly, like a deepsea diver caught in an implosion, like an orange in a squeezer, the spatial limits in which it existed were reduced. A spherical locus in space enclosed it, diminished.

The thing was drawn in and in. The ungrown stumps of its legs folded against its thick torso. The head ducked down against the chest to escape the unrelenting pressure. For a single instant it gathered its enormous perverted power and fought back. Joan was disconcerted, momentarily nauseated, by the backwash of evil.

But Howe withstood it without change of expression; the sphere shrank again.

The eyeless skull split. At once, the sphere shrank to the least possible dimension. A twenty-inch ball hung in the air, a ball whose repulsive superficial details did not invite examination.

Howe held the harmless, disgusting mess in place with a fraction of his mind, and inquired—*"Are you all right, my dear?"*

—*"Yes, Senior. Master Ling helped me once when I needed it."*

—*"That I anticipated. Now for the others."* Speaking aloud he said, "Which do you prefer: To join your leader, or to forget what you know?" He grasped air with his fingers and made a squeezing gesture.

The man with the cigar screamed.

"I take that to be an answer," said Howe. "Very well, Joan, pass them to me, one at a time."

He operated subtly on their minds, smoothing out the patterns of colloidal gradients established by their corporal experience.

A few minutes later the room contained four sane but infant adults—and a gory mess on the rug.

Coburn stepped into a room to which he had not been invited. "School's out, boys," he announced cheerfully. He pointed a finger at one occupant. "That goes for you." Flame crackled from his finger tip, lapped over his adversary. "Yes, and for you." The flames spouted forth a second time. "And for you." A third received his final cleansing.

Brother Artemis, "God's Angry Man," faced the television pick-up. "And if these things be not true," he thundered, "then may the Lord strike me down dead!"

The coroner's verdict of heart failure did not fully account for the charred condition of his remains.

A political rally adjourned early because the principal speaker failed to show up. An anonymous beggar was found collapsed over his pencils and chewing gum. A director of nineteen major corporations caused his secretary to have hysterics by breaking off in the midst of dictating to converse with the empty air before lapsing into cheerful idiocy. A celebrated stereo and television star disappeared. Obituary stories were hastily dug out and completed for seven members of Congress, several judges, and two governors.

The usual evening sing at Camp Mark Twain took place that night without the presence of Camp Director Moulton. He was attending a full conference of the adepts, assembled all in the flesh for the first time in many years.

Joan looked around as she entered the hall. "Where is Master Ling?" she inquired of Howe.

He studied her face for a moment. For the first time since she had first met him nearly two years before she thought he seemed momentarily at a loss. "My dear," he said gently, "you must have realized that Master Ling remained with us, not for his own benefit, but for ours. The crisis for which he waited has been met; the rest of the work we must do alone."

A hand went to her throat. "You . . . you mean . . .?"

"He was very old and very weary. He had kept his heart beating, his body functioning, by continuous control for these past forty-odd years."

"But why did he not renew and regenerate?"

"He did not wish it. We could not expect him to remain here indefinitely after he had grown up."

"No." She bit her trembling lip. "No. That is true. We are children and he has other things to do . . . but—Oh, Ling! Ling! Master Ling!" She buried her head on Howe's shoulder.

—"*Why are you weeping, Little Flower?*"

Her head jerked up.—"*Master Ling!*"

—"*Can that not be which has been? Is there past or future? Have you learned my lessons so poorly? Am I not now with you, as always?*" She felt in the thought the vibrant timeless merriment, the gusto for living which was the hallmark of the gentle Chinese.

With a part of her mind she squeezed Howe's hand.

"Sorry," she said. "I was wrong." She relaxed as Ling had taught her, let her consciousness flow in the revery which encompasses time in a single deathless now.

Howe, seeing that she was at peace, turned his attention to the meeting.

He reached out with his mind and gathered them together into the telepathic network of full conference.—*"I think that you all know why we meet,"* he thought.—*"I have served my time; we enter another and more active period when other qualities than mine are needed. I have called you to consider and pass on my selection of a successor."*

Huxley was finding the thought messages curiously difficult to follow. I must be exhausted from the effort, he thought to himself.

But Howe was thinking aloud again.—*"So be it; we are agreed."* He looked at Huxley. *"Philip, will you accept the trust?"*

"What?!!"

"You are Senior now—by common consent."

"But . . . but . . . I am not ready."

"We think so," answered Howe evenly. "Your talents are needed now. You will grow under responsibility."

—*"Chin up, pal!"* It was Coburn, in private message.

—*"It's all right, Phil."* Joan, that time.

For an instant he seemed to hear Ling's dry chuckle, his calm acceptance.

"I will try!" he answered.

On the last day of camp Joan sat with Mrs. Draper on a terrace of the Home on Shasta, overlooking the valley. She sighed. Mrs. Draper looked up from her knitting and smiled. "Are you sad that the camp is over?"

"Oh, no! I'm glad it is."

"What is it, then?"

"I was just thinking . . . we go to all this effort and trouble to put on this camp. Then we have to fight to keep it safe. Tomorrow those boys go home—then they must be watched, each one of them, while they grow strong enough to protect themselves against all the evil things there are still in the

orld. Next year there will be another crop of boys, and then
nother, and then another. Isn't there any end to it?"

"Certainly there is an end to it. Don't you remember, in
e ancient records, what became of the elders? When we
ave done what there is for us to do here, we move on to
here there is more to do. The human race was not meant
stay here forever."

"It still seems endless."

"It does, when you think of it that way, my dear. The way
make it seem short and interesting is to think about what
ou are going to do next. For example, what are you going
do next?"

"Me?" Joan looked perplexed. Her face cleared. "Why . . .
hy I'm going to get married!"

"I thought so." Mrs. Draper's needles clicked away.

CHAPTER THIRTEEN

"—AND THE TRUTH SHALL MAKE YOU FREE!"

THE GLOBE STILL SWUNG AROUND THE SUN. The seasons came and the seasons went. The sun still shone on the mountainsides; the hills were green, and the valleys lush. The river sought the bosom of the sea, then rode the cloud, and found the hills as rain. The cattle cropped in the brown plains, the fox stalked the hare through the brush. The tides answered the sway of the moon, and the gulls picked at the wet sand in the wake of the tide. The earth was fair and the earth was full; it teemed with life, swarmed with life, overflowed with life—a stream in spate.

Nowhere was man.

Seek the high hills; search him in the plains. Hunt for his spoor in the green jungles; call for him; shout for him. Follow where he has been in the bowels of earth; plumb the dim deep of the sea.

Man is gone; his house stands empty; the door open.

A great ape, with a brain too big for his need and a spirit that troubled him, left his tribe and sought the quiet of the high place that lay above the jungle. He climbed it, hour after hour, urged on by a need that he half understood. He reached a resting place, high above the green trees of his home, higher than any of his tribe had ever climbed. There he found a broad flat stone warm in the sun. He lay down upon it and slept.

But his sleep was troubled. He dreamed strange dreams, unlike anything he knew. They woke him and left him with an aching head.

It would be many generations before one of his line could understand what was left there by those who had departed.

THE END

JERRY WAS A MAN

DON'T BLAME THE MARTIANS. The human race would have developed plasto-biology in any case.

Look at the older registered Kennel Club breeds—glandular giants like the St. Bernard and the Great Dane, silly little atrocities like the Chihuahua and the Pekingese. Consider fancy goldfish.

The damage was done when Dr. Morgan produced new breeds of fruit flies by kicking around their chromosomes with X-ray. After that, the third generation of the Hiroshima survivors did not teach us anything new; those luckless monstrosities merely publicized standard genetic knowledge.

Mr. and Mrs. Bronson van Vogel did not have special reform in mind when they went to the Phoenix Breeding Ranch; Mr. van Vogel simply wanted to buy a Pegasus. He had mentioned it at breakfast. "Are you tied up this morning, my dear?"

"Not especially. Why?"

"I'd like to run out to Arizona and order a Pegasus designed."

"A Pegasus? A flying horse? Why, my sweet?"

He grinned. "Just for fun. Pudgy Dodge was around the Club yesterday with a six-legged dachshund—must have been over a yard long. It was clever, but he swanked so much I want to give him something to stare at. Imagine, Martha—me landing on the Club 'copter platform on a winged horse. That'll snap his eyes back!"

She turned her eyes from the Jersey shore to look indulgently at her husband. She was not fooled; this would be expensive. But Brownie was such a dear! "When do we start?"

113

They landed two hours earlier than they started. The air-sign read, in letters fifty feet high:

PHOENIX BREEDING RANCH
Controlled Genetics—licensed Labor Contractors

" 'Labor Contractors'?" she read. "I thought this place was used just to burbank new animals?"

"They both design and produce," he explained importantly. "They distribute through the mother corporation 'Workers'. You ought to know; you own a big chunk of Workers common."

"You mean I own a bunch of apes? Really?"

"Perhaps I didn't tell you. Haskell and I—" He leaned forward and informed the field that he would land manually; he was a bit proud of his piloting.

He switched off the robot and added, briefly as his attention was taken up by heading the ship down, "Haskell and I have been plowing your General Atomics dividends back into Workers, Inc. Good diversification—still plenty of dirty work for the anthropoids to do." He slapped the keys; the scream of the nose jets stopped conversation.

Bronson had called the manager in flight; they were met—not with red carpet, canopy, and footmen, though the manager strove to give that impression. "Mr. van Vogel? And *Mrs.* van Vogel! We are honored indeed!" He ushered them into a tiny, luxurious unicar; they jeeped off the field, up a ramp, and into the lobby of the administration building. The manager, Mr. Blakesly, did not relax until he had seated them around a fountain in the lounge of his offices, struck cigarettes for them, and provided tall, cool drinks.

Bronson van Vogel was bored by the attention, as it was obviously inspired by his wife's Dun & Bradstreet rating (ten stars, a sunburst, and heavenly music). He preferred people who could convince him that he had invented the Briggs fortune, instead of marrying it.

"This is business Blakesly. I've an order for you."

"So? Well, our facilities are at your disposal. What would you like, sir?"

"I want you to make me a Pegasus."

"A Pegasus? A flying horse?"

"Exactly."

Blakesly pursed his lips. "You seriously want a horse that will fly? An animal like the mythical Pegasus?"

"Yes, yes—that's what I said."

"You embarrass me, Mr. van Vogel. I assume you want a unique gift for your lady. How about a midget elephant, twenty inches high, perfectly housebroken, and able to read and write? He holds the stylus in his trunk—very cunning."

"Does he talk?" demanded Mrs. van Vogel.

"Well, now, my dear lady, his voice box, you know—and his tongue—he was not designed for speech. If you insist on it, I will see what our plasticians can do."

"Now, Martha—"

"You can have your Pegasus, Brownie, but I think I may want this toy elephant. May I see him?"

"Most surely. Hartstone!"

The air answered Blakesly. "Yes, boss?"

"Bring Napoleon to my lounge."

"Right away, sir."

"Now about your Pegasus, Mr. van Vogel . . . I see difficulties but I need expert advice. Dr. Cargrew is the real heart of this organization, the most eminent bio-designer—of terrestrial origin, of course—on the world today." He raised his voice to actuate relays. "Dr. Cargrew!"

"What is it, Mr. Blakesly?"

"Doctor, will you favor me by coming to my office?"

"I'm busy. Later."

Mr. Blakesly excused himself, went into his inner office, then returned to say that Dr. Cargrew would be in shortly. In the mean time Napoleon showed up. The proportions of his noble ancestors had been preserved in miniature; he looked like a statuette of an elephant, come amazingly to life.

He took three measured steps into the lounge, then saluted

115

them each with his trunk. In saluting Mrs. van Vogel he
dropped on his knees as well.

"Oh, how cute!" she gurgled. "Come here, Napoleon."

The elephant looked at Blakesly, who nodded. Napoleon
ambled over and laid his trunk across her lap. She scratched
his ears; he moaned contentedly.

"Show the lady how you can write," ordered Blakesly.
"Fetch your things from my room."

Napoleon waited while she finished treating a particularly
satisfying itch, then oozed away to return shortly with several
sheets of heavy white paper and an oversize pencil. He spread
a sheet in front of Mrs. van Vogel, held it down daintily with
a fore foot, grasped the pencil with his trunk finger, and
printed in large, shaky letters, "I LIKE YOU."

"The darling!" She dropped to her knees and put her arms
around his neck. "I simply must have him. How much is
he?"

"Napoleon is part of a limited edition of six," Blakesly
said carefully. "Do you want an exclusive model, or may the
others be sold?"

"Oh, I don't care. I just want Nappie. Can I write him a
note?"

"Certainly, Mrs. van Vogel. Print large letters and use
Basic English. Napoleon knows most of it. His price, non-
exclusive is $350,000. That includes five years salary for his
attending veterinary."

"Give the gentleman a check, Brownie," she said over her
shoulder.

"But Martha—"

"Don't be tiresome, Brownie." She turned back to her pet
and began printing. She hardly looked up when Dr. Cargrew
came in.

Cargrew was a chilly figure in white overalls and skull
cap. He shook hands brusquely, struck a cigarette and sat
down. Blakesly explained.

Cargrew shook his head. "It's a physical impossibility."

Van Vogel stood up. "I can see," he said distantly, "That

should have taken my custom to NuLife Laboratories. I came here because we have a financial interest in this firm and because I was naive enough to believe the claims of your advertisements."

"Siddown, young man!" Cargrew ordered. "Take your trade to those thumb-fingered idiots if you wish—but I warn you they couldn't grow wings on a grasshopper. First you listen to me.

"We can grow anything and make it live. I can make you a living thing—I won't call it an animal—the size and shape of that table over there. It wouldn't be good for anything, but it would be alive. It would ingest food, use chemical energy, give off excretions, and display irritability. But it would be a silly piece of manipulation. Mechanically a table and an animal are two different things. Their functions are different, so their shapes are different. Now I can make you a winged horse—"

"You just said you couldn't."

"Don't interrupt. I can make a winged horse that will look just like the pictures in the fairy stories. If you want to pay for it; we'll make it—we're in business. But it won't be able to fly."

"Why not?"

"Because it's not built for flying. The ancient who dreamed up that myth knew nothing about aerodynamics and still less about biology. He stuck wings on a horse, just stuck them on, thumb tacks and glue. But that doesn't make a flying machine. Remember, son, that an animal is a machine, primarily a heat engine with a control system to operate levers and hydraulic systems, according to definite engineering laws. You savvy aerodynamics?"

"Well, I'm a pilot."

"Hummph! Well, try to understand this. A horse hasn't got the heat engine for flight. He's a hayburner and that's not efficient. We might mess around with a horse's insides so that he could live on a diet of nothing but sugar and then he might have enough energy to fly short distances. But he

still would not look like the mythical Pegasus. To anchor hi
flying muscles he would need a breast bone maybe ten fee
long. He might have to have as much as eighty feet wing
spread. Folded, his wings would cover him like a tent. You'r¢
up against the cube-square disadvantage."

"Huh?"

Cargrew gestured impatiently. "Lift goes by the square o
a given dimension; dead load by the cube of the same dimen
sion, other things being equal. I might be able to make yo¤
a Pegasus the size of a cat without distorting the proportion;
too much."

"No, I want one I can ride. I don't mind the wing sprea¢
and I'll put up with the big breast bone. When can I hav¢
him?"

Cargrew looked disgusted, shrugged, and replied, "I'l¤
have to consult with B'na Kreeth." He whistled and chirped
a portion of the wall facing them dissolved and they found
themselves looking into a laboratory. A Martian, life-size
showed in the forepart of the three-dimensional picture.

When the creature chirlupped back at Cargrew, Mrs. var
Vogel looked up, then quickly looked away. She knew it was
silly but she simply could not stand the sight of Martians—
and the ones who had modified themselves to a semi-manlik¢
form disgusted her the most.

After they had twittered and gestured at each other for ¿
minute or two Cargrew turned back to van Vogel. "B'na
says that you should forget it; it would take too long. H¢
wants to know how you'd like a fine unicorn, or a pair, guaranteed to breed true?"

"Unicorns are old hat. How long would the Pegasus take?"

After another squeaky-door conversation Cargrew
answered, "Ten years probably, sixteen years on the guar-
antee."

"Ten years? That's ridiculous!"

Cargrew looked shirty. "*I* thought it would take fifty, bu¤
if B'na says that he can do it three to five generations, ther
he can do it. B'na is the finest bio-micrurgist in two planets

118

His chromosome surgery is unequalled. After all, young man, natural processes would take upwards of a million years to achieve the same result, if it were achieved at all. Do you expect to be able to buy miracles?"

Van Vogel had the grace to look sheepish. "Excuse me, Doctor. Let's forget it. Ten years really is too long. How about the other possibility? You said you could make a picture-book Pegasus, as long as I did not insist on flight. Could I ride him? On the ground?"

"Oh, certainly. No good for polo, but you could ride him."

"I'll settle for that. Ask Benny creeth, or what ever his name is, how long it would take."

The Martian had faded out of the screens. "I don't need to ask him," Cargrew asserted. "This is my job—purely manipulation. B'na's collaboration is required only for rearrangement and transplanting of genes—true genetic work. I can let you have the beast in eighteen months."

"Can't you do better than that?"

"What do you expect, man? It takes eleven months to grow a new-born colt. I want one month of design and planning. The embryo will be removed on the fourth day and will be developed in an extra-uterine capsule. I'll operate ten or twelve times during gestation, grafting and budding and other things you've heard of. One year from now we'll have a baby colt, with wings. Thereafter I'll deliver to you a six-months-old Pegasus."

. "I'll take it."

Cargrew made some notes, then read, "One alate horse, not capable of flight and not to breed true. Basic breed your choice—I suggest a Palomino, or an Arabian. Wings designed after a condor, in white. Simulated pin feathers with a grafted fringe of quill feathers, or reasonable facsimile." He passed the sheet over. "Initial that and we'll start in advance of formal contract."

"It's a deal," agreed van Vogel. "What is the fee?" He placed his monogram under Cargrew's.

Cargrew made further notes and handed them to

Blakesly—estimates of professional man-hours, technician man-hours, purchases, and overhead. He had padded the figures to subsidize his collateral research but even he raised his eyebrows at the dollars-and-cents interpretation Blakesly put on the data. "That will be an even two million dollars."

Van Vogel hesitated; his wife had looked up at the mention of money. But she turned her attention back to the scholarly elephant.

Blakesly added hastily, "That is for an exclusive creation, of course."

"Naturally," van Vogel agreed briskly, and added the figure to the memorandum.

Van Vogel was ready to return, but his wife insisted on seeing the "apes", as she termed the anthropoid workers. The discovery that she owned a considerable share in these sub-human creatures had intrigued her. Blakesly eagerly suggested a trip through the laboratories in which the workers were developed from true apes.

They were arranged in seven buildings, the seven "Days of Creation". "First Day" was a large building occupied by Cargrew, his staff, his operating rooms, incubators, and laboratories. Martha van Vogel stared in horrified fascination at living organs and even complete embryos, living artificial lives sustained by clever class and metal recirculating systems and exquisite automatic machinery.

She could not appreciate the techniques; it seemed depressing. She had about decided against plasto-biology when Napoleon, by tugging at her skirts, reminded her that it produced good things as well as horrors.

The building "Second Day" they did not enter; it was occupied by B'na Kreeth and his racial colleagues. "We could not stay alive in it, you understand," Blakesly explained. Van Vogel nodded; his wife hurried on—she wanted no Martians, even behind plastiglass.

From there on the buildings were for development and production of commercial workers. "Third Day" was used for the development of variations in the anthropoids to meet constantly changing labor requirements. "Fourth Day" was a very large building devoted entirely to production-line incubators for commercial types of anthropoids. Blakesly explained that they had dispensed with normal birth. "The policy permits exact control of forced variations, such as for size, and saves hundreds of thousands of worker-hours on the part of the female anthropoids."

Martha van Vogel was delighted with "Fifth Day", the anthropoid kindergarten where the little tykes learned to talk and were conditioned to the social patterns necessary to their station in life. They worked at simple tasks such as sorting buttons and digging holes in sand piles, with pieces of candy given as incentives for fast and accurate work.

"Six Day" completed the anthropoids' educations. Each learned the particular sub-trade it would practice, cleaning, digging, and especially agricultural semi-skills such as weeding, thinning, and picking. "One Nisei farmer working three neo-chimpanzees can grow as many vegetables as a dozen old-style farm hands," Blakesly asserted. "They really *like* to work—when we get through with them."

They admired the almost incredibly heavy tasks done by modified gorillas and stopped to gaze at the little neo-Capuchins doing high picking on prop trees, then moved on toward "Seventh Day."

This building was used for the radioactive mutation of genes and therefore located some distance away from the others. They had to walk, as the sidewalk was being repaired; the detour took them past workers' pens and barracks. Some of the anthropoids crowded up to the wire and began calling to them: "Sigret! Sigret! Preese, Missy! Preese, Boss! Sigret!"

"What are they saying?" Martha van Vogel inquired.

"They are asking for cigarettes," Blakesly answered in annoyed tones. "They know better, but they are like children. Here—I'll put a stop to it." He stepped up to the wire and shouted to an elderly male, "Hey! Strawboss!"

The worker addressed wore, in addition to the usual short canvas kilt, a bedraggled arm band. He turned and shuffled toward the fence. "Strawboss," ordered Blakesly, "get those Joes away from here."

"Okay, Boss," the old fellow acknowledged and started cuffing those nearest him. "Scram, you Joes! Scram!"

"But I have some cigarettes," protested Mrs. van Vogel, "and I would gladly have given them some."

"It doesn't do to pamper them," the Manager told her. "They have been taught that luxuries come only from work. I must apologize for my poor children; those in these pens are getting old and forgetting their manners."

She did not answer but moved further along the fence to where one old neo-chimp was pressed up against the wire, staring at them with soft, tragic eyes, like a child at a bakery window. He had taken no part in the jostling demand for tobacco and had been let alone by the strawboss. "Would you like a cigarette?" she asked him.

"Preese, Missy."

She struck one which he accepted with fumbling grace, took a long, lung-filling drag, let the smoke trickle out his nostrils, and said shyly, "Sankoo, Missy. Me Jerry."

"How do you do, Jerry?"

"Howdy, Missy." He bobbed down, bending his knees, ducking his head, and clasping his hands to his chest, all in one movement.

"Come along, Martha." Her husband and Blakesly had moved in behind her.

"In a moment," she answered. "Brownie, meet my friend Jerry. Doesn't he look just like Uncle Albert? Except that he looks so sad. Why are you unhappy, Jerry?"

"They don't understand abstract ideas," put in Blakesly.

But Jerry surprised him. "Jerry sad," he announced in tones so doleful that Martha van Vogel did not know whether to laugh or cry.

"Why, Jerry?" she asked gently. "Why are you so sad?"

"No work," he stated. "No sigret. No candy. No work."

"These are all old workers who have passed their useful-

122

ness," Blakesly repeated. "Idleness upsets them, but we have nothing for them to do."

"Well!" she said. "Then why don't you have them sort buttons, or something like that, such as the baby ones do?"

"They wouldn't even do that properly," Blakesly answered her. "These workers are senile."

"Jerry isn't senile! You heard him talk."

"Well, perhaps not. Just a moment." He turned to the apeman, who was squatting down in order to scratch Napoleon's head with a long forefinger thrust through the fence. "You, Joe! Come here."

Blakesly felt around the worker's hairy neck and located a thin steel chain to which was attached a small metal tag. He studied it. "You're right," he admitted. "He's not really over age, but his eyes are bad. I remember the lot—cataracts as a result of an unfortunate linked mutation." He shrugged.

"But that's no reason to let him grieve his heart out in idleness."

"Really, Mrs. van Vogel, you should not upset yourself about it. They don't stay in these pens long—only a few days at the most."

"Oh," she answered, somewhat mollified, "you have some other place to retire them to, then. Do you give them something to do there? You should—Jerry wants to work. Don't you, Jerry?"

The neo-chimp had been struggling to follow the conversation. He caught the last idea and grinned. "Jerry work! Sure mike! Good worker." He flexed his fingers, then made fists, displaying fully opposed thumbs.

Mr. Blakesly seemed somewhat nonplused. "Really, Mrs. van Vogel, there is no need. You see—" He stopped.

Van Vogel had been listening irritably. His wife's enthusiasms annoyed him, unless they were also his own. Furthermore he was beginning to blame Blakesly for his own recent extravagance and had a premonition that his wife would find some way to make him pay, very sweetly, for his indulgence.

Being annoyed with both of them, he chucked in the perfect wrong remark. "Don't be silly, Martha. They don't retire them; they liquidate them."

It took a little time for the idea to soak in, but when it did she was furious. "Why . . . why—I never heard of such a thing! You ought to be ashamed. You . . . you would shoot your own grandmother."

"Mrs. van Vogel—please!"

"Don't 'Mrs. van Vogel' me! It's got to stop—you hear me?" She looked around at the death pens, at the milling hundreds of old workers therein. "It's horrible. You work them until they can't work anymore, then you take away their little comforts, and you *dispose* of them. I wonder you don't eat them!"

"They do," her husband said brutally. "Dog food."

"What! Well, we'll put a stop to that!"

"Mrs. van Vogel," Blakesly pleaded. "Let me explain."

"Hummph! Go ahead. It had better be good."

"Well, it's like this—" His eye fell on Jerry, standing with worried expression at the fence. "Scram, Joe!" Jerry shuffled away.

"Wait, Jerry!" Mrs. van Vogel called out. Jerry paused uncertainly. "Tell him to come back," she ordered Blakesly.

The Manager bit his lip, then called out, "Come back here."

He was beginning definitely to dislike Mrs. van Vogel, despite his automatic tendency to genuflect in the presence of a high credit rating. To be told how to run his own business—well, now, indeed! "Mrs. van Vogel, I admire your humanitarian spirit but you don't understand the situation. We understand our workers and do what is best for them. They die painlessly before their disabilities can trouble them. They live happy lives, happier than yours or mine. We trim off the bad parts of their lives, nothing more. And don't forget, these poor beasts would never have been born had we not arranged it."

She shook her head. "Fiddlesticks! You'll be quoting the

Bible at me next. There will be no more of it, Mr. Blakesly.
I shall hold you personally responsible."

Blakesly looked bleak. "My responsibilities are to the directors."

"You think so?" She opened her purse and snatched out her telephone. So great was her agitation that she did not bother to call through, but signalled the local relay operator instead. "Phoenix? Get me Great New York Murray Hill 9Q-4004, Mr. Haskell. Priority—star subscriber 777. Make it quick." She stood there, tapping her foot and glaring, until her business manager answered. "Haskell? This is Martha van Vogel. How much Workers, Incorporated, common do I own? No, no, never mind that—what percent? . . . so? Well, it's not enough. I want 51% by tomorrow morning . . . all right, get proxies for the rest but get it . . . I didn't ask you what it would cost; I said to get it. Get busy." She disconnected abruptly and turned to her husband. "We're leaving, Brownie, and we are taking Jerry with us. Mr. Blakesly, will you kindly have him taken out of that pen? Give him a check for the amount, Brownie."

"Now, Martha—"

"My mind is made up, Brownie."

Mr. Blakesly cleared his throat. It was going to be pleasant to thwart this woman. "The workers are never sold. I'm sorry. It's a matter of policy."

"Very well then, I'll take a permanent lease."

"This worker has been removed from the labor market. He is not for lease."

"Am I going to have more trouble with you?"

"If you please, Madame! This worker is not available under any terms—but, as a courtesy to you, I am willing to transfer to you indentures for him, gratis. I want you to know that the policies of this firm are formed from a very real concern for the welfare of our charges as well as from the standpoint of good business practice. We therefore reserve the right to inspect at any time to assure ourselves that you are taking proper care of this worker." There, he told himse savagely, that will stop her clock!

"Of course. Thank you, Mr. Blakesly. You are most gra cious."

The trip back to Great New Nork was not jolly. Napoleo hated it and let it be known. Jerry was patient but airsic By the time they grounded the van Vogels were not on speaing terms.

"I'm sorry, Mrs. van Vogel. The shares were simply ne available. We should have had proxy on the O'Toole blo but someone tied them up an hour before I reached them.

"Blakesly."

"Undoubtedly. You should not have tipped him off; yo gave him time to warn his employers."

"Don't waste time telling me what mistakes I made ye terday. What are you going to do today?"

"Mr. dear Mrs. van Vogel, what can I do? I'll carry ou any instructions you care to give."

"Don't talk nonsense. You are supposed to be smarte than I am; that's why I pay you to do my thinking for me.

Mr. Haskell looked helpless.

His pincipal struck a cigarette so hard she broke it. "Wh isn't Weinberg here?"

"Really, Mrs. van Vogel, there are no special legal aspect You want the stock; we can't buy it nor bind it. There fore—"

"I pay Weinberg to know the legal angles. Get him."

Weinberg was leaving his office; Haskell caught him o a chase-me circuit. "Sidney," Haskell called out. "Come my office, will you? Oscar Haskell."

"Sorry. How about four o'clock?"

"Sidney, I want you—now!" cut in the client's voice. "Th is Martha van Vogel."

The little man shrugged helplessly. "Right away," agreed. That woman—why hadn't he retired on his ol hundred and twenty-fifth birthday, as his wife had urged him to?

Ten minutes later he was listening to Haskell's explanations and his client's interruptions. When they had finished he spread his hands. "What do you expect, Mrs. van Vogel? These workers are chattels. You have not been able to buy the property rights involved; you are stopped. But I don't see what you are worked up about. They gave you the worker whose life you wanted preserved.

She spoke forcefully under her breath, then answered him. 'That's not important. What is one worker among millions? I want to stop this killing, all of it."

Weinberg shook his head. "If you were able to prove that their methods of disposing of these beasts were inhumane, or that they were negligent of their physical welfare before destroying them, or that the destruction was wanton—"

"Wanton? It certain is!"

"Probably not in a legal sense, my dear lady. There was a case, Julius Hartman et al. vs. Hartman Estate, 1972, I believe, in which a permanent injunction was granted against carrying out a term of the will which called for the destruction of a valuable collection of Persian cats. But in order to use that theory you would have to show that these creatures, when superannuated, are notwithstanding more valuable alive than dead. You cannot compel a person to maintain chattels at a loss."

"See here, Sidney, I didn't get you over here to tell me how this can't be done. If what I want isn't legal, then get a law passed."

Weinberg looked at Haskell, who looked embarrassed and answered, "Well, the fact of the matter is, Mrs. van Vogel, that we have agreed with the other members of the Commonwealth Association not to subsidize any legislation during the incumbency of the present administration."

"How ridiculous! Why?"

"The Legislative Guild has brought out a new fair-practices code which we consider quite unfair, a sliding scale which penalizes the well-to-do—all very nice sounding, with special provisions for nominal fees for veterans' private bills and such things—but in fact the code is confiscatory. Even the Briggs Foundation can hardly afford to take a proper interest in public affairs under this so-called code."

"Hmmph! A fine day when legislators join unions—they are professional men. Bribes should be competitive. Get an injunction."

"Mrs. van Vogel," protested Weinberg, "how can you expect me to get an injuction against an organization which has no legal existence? In a legal sense, there is no Legislative Guild, just as the practice of assisting legislation by subsidy has itself no legal existence."

"And babies come under cabbage leaves. Quit stalling me, gentlemen. What are you going to do?"

Weinberg spoke when he saw that Haskell did not intend to. "Mrs. van Vogel, I think we should retain a special shyster."

"I don't employ shysters, even—I don't understand the way they think. I am a simple housewife, Sidney."

Mr. Weinberg flinched at her self-designation while noting that he must not let her find out that the salary of his own staff shyster was charged to her payroll. As convention required, he maintained the front of a simple, barefoot solicitor, but he had found out long ago that Martha van Vogel's problems required an occasional dose of the more exotic branch of the law. "The man I have in mind is a creative artist," he insisted. "It is no more necessary to understand him than it is to understand the composer in order to appreciate a symphony. I do recommend that you talk with him, at least."

"Oh, very well! Get him up here."

"Here? My dear lady!" Haskell was shocked at the suggestion; Weinberg looked amazed. "It would not only cause any action you bring to be thrown out of court if it were known that you had consulted this man, but it would prejudice any Briggs enterprise for years."

Mrs. van Vogel shrugged. "You men. I never will understand the way you think. Why shouldn't one consult a shyster as openly as one consults an astrologer?"

James Roderick McCoy was not a large man, but he seemed large. He managed to dominate even so large a room as Mrs. van Vogel's salon. His business card read:

J. R. McCoy
"The Real McCoy"

Licensed Shyster—Fixing, Special Contacts,
Angles. All Work Guaranteed.

Telephone Skyline 9-8M4554
Ask for Mac

The number given was the pool room of the notorious Three Planets Club. He wasted no time on offices and kept his files in his head—the only safe place for them.

He was sitting on the floor, attempting to teach Jerry to shoot craps, while Mrs. van Vogel explained her problem. "What do you think, Mr. McCoy? Could we approach it through the SPCA? My public relations staff could give it a build up."

McCoy got to his feet. "Jerry's eyes aren't so bad; he caught me trying to palm box cars off on him as a natural. No," he continued, "the SPCA angle is no good. It's what 'workers' will expect. They'll be ready to prove that the anthropoids actually enjoy being killed off."

Jerry rattled the dice hopefully. "That's all, Jerry. Scram."

"Okay, Boss." The ape man got to his feet and went to the big stereo which filled a corner of the room. Napoleon ambled after him and switched it on. Jerry punched a selector button and got a blues singer. Napoleon immediately punched another, then another and another until he got a loud but popular band. He stood there, beating out the rhythm with his trunk.

Jerry looked pained and switched it back to his blues singer. Napoleon stubbornly reached out with his prehensile nose and switched it off.

Jerry used a swear word.

"Boys!" called out Mrs. van Vogel. "Quit squabbling. Jerry, let Nappie play what he wants to. You can play the stereo when Nappie has to take his nap."

"Okay, Missy Boss."

McCoy was interested. "Jerry likes music?"

"Like it? He loves it. He's been learning to sing."

"Huh? This I gotta hear."

"Certainly. Nappie—turn off the stereo." The elephant complied but managed to look put upon. "Now Jerry—'Jingle Bells.' " She led him in it:

"Jingle bells, jingle bells, jingle all the day—", and he followed.

"Jinger bez, jinger bez, jinger awrah day;
Oh, wot fun tiz to ride in one-hoss open sray."

He was flat, he was terrible. He looked ridiculous, patting out the time with one splay foot. But it was singing.

"Say, that's fast!" McCoy commented. "Too bad Nappie can't talk—we'd have a duet."

Jerry looked puzzled. "Nappie talk good," he stated. He bent over the elephant and spoke to him. Napoleon grunted and moaned back at him. "See, Boss?" Jerry said triumphantly.

"What did he say?"

"He say, 'Can Nappie pray stereo now?' "

"Very well, Jerry," Mrs. van Vogel interceded. The ape man spoke to his chum in whispers. Napoleon squealed and did not turn on the stereo.

"Jerry!" said his mistress. "I said nothing of the sort; he does *not* have to play your blues singer. Come away, Jerry. Nappie—play what you want to."

"You mean he tried to cheat?" McCoy inquired with interest.

"He certainly did."

"Hmm—Jerry's got the makings of a real citizen. Shave

him and put shoes on him and he'd get by all right in the precinct I grew up in." He stared at the anthropoid. Jerry stared back, puzzled but patient. Mrs. van Vogel had thrown away the dirty canvas kilt which was both his badge of servitude and a concession to propriety and had replaced it with a kilt in the bright Cameron war plaid, complete to sporan, and topped off with a Glengarry.

"Do you suppose he could learn to play the bagpipes?" McCoy asked. "I'm beginning to get an angle."

"Why, I don't know. What's your idea?"

McCoy squatted down cross-legged and began practicing rolls with his dice. "Never mind," he answered when it suited him, "that angle's no good. But we're getting there." He rolled four naturals, one after the other. "You say Jerry still belongs to the Corporation?"

"In a titular sense, yes. I doubt if they will ever try to repossess him."

"I wish they would try." He scooped up the dice and stood up. "It's in the bag, Sis. Forget it. I'll want to talk to your publicity man but you can quit worrying about it."

Of course Mrs. van Vogel should have knocked before entering her husband's room—but then she would not have overheard what he was saying, nor to whom.

"That's right," she heard him say, "we haven't any further need for him. Take him away, the sooner the better. Just be sure the men you send have a signed order directing us to turn him over."

She was not apprehensive, as she did not understand the conversation, but merely curious. She looked over her husband's shoulder at the video screen.

There she saw Blakesly's face. His voice was saying, "Very well, Mr. van Vogel, the anthropoid will be picked up tomorrow."

She strode up to the screen. "Just a minute, Mr. Blakesly—"then, to her husband, "Brownie, what in the world do you think you are doing?"

The expression she surprised on his face was not one he had ever let her see before. "Why don't you knock?"

"Maybe it's a good thing I didn't. Brownie, did I hear you right. Were you telling Mr. Blakesly to pick up Jerry?" She turned to the screen. "Was that it, Mr. Blakesly?"

"That is correct, Mrs. van Vogel. And I must say I find this confusion most—"

"Stow it." She turned back. "Brownie, what have you to say for yourself?"

"Martha, you are being preposterous. Between that elephant and that ape this place is a zoo. I actually caught your precious Jerry smoking my special, personal cigars today . . not to mention the fact that both of them play the stereo all day long until a man can't get a moment's peace. I certainly don't have to stand for such things in my own house."

"Whose house, Brownie?"

"That's beside the point. I will not stand for—"

"Never mind." She turned to the screen. "My husband seems to have lost his taste for exotic animals, Mr. Blakesly Cancel the order for a Pegasus."

"Martha!"

"Sauce for the goose, Brownie. I'll pay for your whims I'm damned if I'll pay for your tantrums. The contract is cancelled, Mr. Blakesly. Mr. Haskell will arrange the details."

Blakesly shrugged. "Your capricious behavior will cost you, of course. The penalties—"

"I said Mr. Haskell would arrange the details. One more thing, Mister Manager Blakesly—have you done as I told you to?"

"What do you mean?"

"You know what I mean—are those poor creatures still alive and well?"

"That is not your business." He had, in fact, suspended the killings; the directors had not wanted to take any chances until they saw what the Briggs trust could manage, but Blakesly would not give her the satisfaction of knowing.

She looked at him as if he were a skipped dividend. "It's

ot, eh? Well, bear this in mind, you cold-blooded little pip-queak: I'm holding you personally responsible. If just one f them dies from *anything*, I'll have your skin for a rug." She ipped off the connection and turned to her husband. Brownie—"

"It's useless to say anything," he cut in, in the cold voice e normally used to bring her to heel. "I shall be at the Club. ood-bye!"

"That's just what I was going to suggest."

"What?"

"I'll have your clothes sent over. Do you have anything lse in this house?"

He stared at her. "Don't talk like a fool, Martha."

"I'm not talking like a fool." She looked him up and down. My, but you are handsome, Brownie. I guess I was a fool think I could buy a big hunk of man with a checkbook. I uess a girl gets them free, or she doesn't get them at all. hanks for the lesson." She turned and slammed out of the oom and into her own suite.

Five minutes later, makeup repaired and nerves steadied y a few whiffs of Fly-Right, she called the pool room of the hree Planets Club. McCoy came to the screen carrying a ue. "Oh, it's you, sugar puss. Well, snap it up—I've got ur bits on this game."

"This is business."

"Okay, okay—spill it."

She told him the essentials. "I'm sorry about cancelling e flying horse contract, Mr. McCoy. I hope it won't make ur job any harder. I'm afraid I lost my temper."

"Fine. Go lose it again."

"Huh?"

"You're barrelling down the groove, kid. Call Blakesly up ain. Bawl him out. Tell him to keep his bailiffs away from u, or you'll stuff 'em and use them for hat racks. Dare him take Jerry away from you."

"I don't understand you."

"You don't have to, girlie. Remember this: You can't have

133

a bull fight until you get the bull mad enough to fight. Ha
Weinberg get a temporary injunction restraining Worker
Incorporated, from reclaiming Jerry. Have your boss pre
agent give me a buzz. Then you call in the newsboys and te
them what you think of Blakesly. Make it nasty. Tell the
you intend to put a stop to this wholesale murder if it tak
every cent you've got."

"Well . . . all right. Will you come to see me before I ta
to them?"

"Nope—gotta get back to my game. Tomorrow, mayb
Don't fret about having cancelled that silly winged-hors
deal. I always did think your old man was weak in the hea
and it's saved you a nice piece of change. You'll need it whe
I send in my bill. Boy, am I going to clip you! Bye now."

The bright letters trailed around the sides of the Tim
Building: "WORLD'S RICHEST WOMAN PUTS U
FIGHT FOR APE MAN." On the giant video screen abov
showed a transcribe of Jerry, in his ridiculous Highland chi
outfit. A small army of police surrounded the Briggs tow
house, while Mrs. van Vogel informed anyone who woul
listen, including several news services, that she would defer
Jerry personally and to the death.

The public relations office of Workers, Incorporate
denied any intention of seizing Jerry; the denial got nowher

In the meantime technicians installed extra audio ar
video circuits in the largest court room in town, for one Jer
(no surname), described as a legal, permanent resident
these United States, had asked for a permanent injuncti
against the corporate person "Workers," its officers, emplo
ees, successors, or assignees, forbidding it to do him ar
physical harm and in particular forbidding it to kill him.

Through his attorney, the honorable and distinguish
and stuffily respectable Augustus Pomfrey, Jerry broug
the action *in his own name*.

Martha van Vogel sat in the court room as a spectat

nly, but she was surrounded by secretaries, guards, maid,
·ublicity men, and yes men, and had one television camera
rained on her alone. She was nervous. McCoy had insisted
n briefing Pomfrey through Weinberg, to keep Pomfrey
·om knowing that he was being helped by a shyster. She
·ad her own opinion of Pomfrey—

Then McCoy had insisted that Jerry not wear his beautiful
·ew kilt but had dressed him in faded dungaree trousers and
·cket. It seemed poor theater to her.

Jerry himself worried her. He seemed confused by the
·ghts and the noise and the crowd, about to go to pieces.

And McCoy had refused to go to the trial with her. He
·ad told her that it was quite impossible, that his mere pres-
·nce would alienate the court, and Weinberg had backed
·im up. Men! Their minds were devious—they seemed to
·ke twisted ways of doing things. It confirmed her opinion
·hat men should not be allowed to vote.

But she felt lost without the immediate presence of McCoy's
·asy self-confidence. Away from him, she wondered why she
·ad ever trusted such an important matter to an irrespon-
·ible, jumping jack, bird-brained clown as McCoy. She
·hewed her nails and wished he were present.

The panel of attorneys appearing for Workers, Incorpor-
·ted, began by moving that the action be dismissed without
·rial, on the theory that Jerry was a chattel of the corpor-
·tion, an integral part of it, and no more able to sue than
·he thumb can sue the brain.

The honorable Augustus Pomfrey looked every inch the
·tatesman as he bowed to the court and to his opponents.
·It is indeed strange," he began, "to hear the second-hand
·oice of a legal fiction, a soulless, imaginary quantity called
· corporate 'person,' argue that a flesh-and-blood creature,
· being of hopes and longings and passions, has not legal
·xistence. I see here beside me my poor cousin Jerry." He
·atted Jerry on the shoulder; the ape man, needing reassur-
·nce, slid a hand into his. It went over well.

"But when I look for this abstract fancy 'Workers,' what

135

do I find? Nothing—some words on paper, some signed bit of foolscap—"

"If the Court please, a question," put in the opposition chief attorney, "does the learned counsel contend that a limited liability stock company cannot own property?"

"Will the counsel reply?" directed the judge.

"Thank you. My esteemed colleague has set up a straw man; I contended only that the question as to whether Jerry is a chattel of Workers, Incorporated, is immaterial, non essential, irrelevant. I am part of the corporate city of Great New York. Does that deny me my civil rights as a person of flesh and blood? In fact it does not even rob me of my right to sue that civic corporation of which I am a part, if, in my opinion, I am wronged by it. We are met today in the mellow light of equity, rather than in the cold and narrow confines of law. It seemed a fit time to dwell on the strange absurdities we live by, whereunder a nonentity of paper and legal fiction could deny the existence of this our poor cousin. I ask that the learned attorneys for the corporation stipulate that Jerry does, in fact, exist, and let us get on with the action."

They huddled; the answer was "No."

"Very well. My client asked to be examined in order that the court may determine his status and being."

"Objection! This anthropoid cannot be examined; he is a mere part and chattel of the respondent."

"That is what we are about to determine," the judge answered dryly. "Objection overruled."

"Go sit in that chair, Jerry."

"Objection! This beast cannot take an oath—it is beyond his comprehension."

"What have you to say to that, Counsel?"

"If it pleases the Court," answered Pomfrey, "the simplest thing to do is to put him in the chair and find out."

"Let him take the stand. The clerk will administer the oath." Martha van Vogel gripped the arms of her chair. McCoy had spent a full week training him for this. Would the poor thing blow up without McCoy to guide him?

136

The clerk droned through the oath; Jerry looked puzzled but patient.

"Your honor," said Pomfrey, "when young children must give testimony, it is customary to permit a little leeway in the wording, to fit their mental attainments. May I be permitted?" He walked up to Jerry.

"Jerry, my boy, are you a good worker?"

"Sure mike! Jerry good worker!"

"Maybe bad worker, huh? Lazy. Hide from strawboss."

"No, no, no! Jerry good worker. Dig. Weed. Not dig up vegetaber. Dig up weed. Work hard."

"You will see," Pomfrey addressed the court, "that my client has very definite ideas of what is true and what is false. Now let us attempt to find out whether or not he has moral values which require him to tell the truth. Jerry—"

"Yes, Boss."

Pomfrey spread his hand in front of the anthropoid's face. "How many fingers do you see?"

Jerry reached out and ticked them off. "One—two—sree—four, uh—five."

"Six fingers, Jerry."

"Five, Boss."

"Six fingers, Jerry. I give you cigarette. Six."

"Five, Boss. Jerry not cheat."

Pomfrey spread his hands. "Will the court accept him?"

The court did. Martha van Vogel sighed. Jerry could not count very well and she had been afraid that he would forget his lines and accept the bribe. But he had been promised all the cigarettes he wanted and chocolate as well if he would remember to insist that five was five.

"I suggest," Pomfrey went on, "that the matter has been established. Jerry is an entity; if he can be accepted as a witness, then surely he may have his day in court. Even a dog may have his day in court. Will my esteemed colleagues stipulate?"

Workers, Incorporated, through its battery of lawyers,

agreed—just in time, for the judge was beginning to cloud up. He had been much impressed by the little performance.

The tide was with him; Pomfrey used it. "If it please the court and if the counsels for the respondent will permit, we can shorten these proceedings. I will state the theory under which relief is sought and then, by a few questions, it may be settled one way or another. I ask that it be stipulated that it was the intention of Workers, Incorporated, through its servants, to take the life of my client."

Stipulation was refused.

"So? Then I ask that the court take judicial notice of the well known fact that these anthropoid workers are destroyed when they no longer show a profit; thereafter I will call witnesses, starting with Horace Blakesly, to show that Jerry was and presumably is under such sentence of death."

Another hurried huddle resulted in the stipulation that Jerry had, indeed, been scheduled for euthanasia.

"Then," said Pomfrey, "I will state my theory. Jerry is not an animal, but a man. It is not legal to kill him—it is murder."

First there was silence, then the crowd gasped. People had grown used to animals that talked and worked, but they were no more prepared to think of them as persons, humans, *men*, than were the haughty Roman citizens prepared to concede human feelings to their barbarian slaves.

Pomfrey let them have it while they were still groggy. "What is a man? A collection of living cells and tissues? A legal fiction, like this corporate 'person' that would take poor Jerry's life? No, a man is none of these things. A man is a collection of hopes and fears, of human longings, of aspirations greater than himself—more than the clay from which he came; less than the Creator which lifted him up from the clay. Jerry has been taken from his jungle and made something more than the poor creatures who were his ancestors, even as you and I. We ask that this Court recognize his manhood."

The opposing attorneys saw that the Court was moved; they drove in fast. An anthropoid, they contended, could not be a man because he lacked human shape and human intelligence. Pomfrey called his first witness—Master B'na Kreeth.

The Martian's normal bad temper had not been improved by being forced to wait around for three days in a travel tank, to say nothing of the indignity of having to interrupt his researches to take part in the childish pow-wows of terrestrials.

There was further delay to irritate him while Pomfrey forced the corporation attorneys to accept B'na as an expert witness. They wanted to refuse but could not—he was their own Director of Research. He also held voting control of all Martian-held Workers' stock, a fact unmentioned but hampering.

More delay while an interpreter was brought in to help administer the oath—B'na Kreeth, self-centered as all Martians, had never bothered to learn English.

He twittered and chirped in answer to the demand that he tell the truth, the whole truth, and so forth; the interpreter looked pained. "He says he can't do it," he informed the judge.

Pomfrey asked for exact translation.

The interpreter looked uneasily at the judge. "He says that if he told the whole truth you fools—not 'fools' exactly; it's a Martian word meaning a sort of headless worm—would not understand it."

The court discussed the idea of contempt briefly. When the Martian understood that he was about to be forced to remain in a travel tank for thirty days he came down off his high horse and agreed to tell the truth as adequately as was possible; he was accepted as a witness.

"Are you a man?" demanded Pomfrey.

"Under your laws and by your standards I am a man."

"By what theory? Your body is unlike ours; you cannot even live in our air. You do not speak our language; your ideas are alien to us. How can you be a man?"

The Martian answered carefully: *"I quote from the Terra-Martian Treaty, which you must accept as supreme law. 'All members of the Great Race, while sojourning on the Third Planet, shall have all the rights and prerogatives of the native dominant race of the Third Planet.' This clause has been interpreted by the Bi-Planet Tribunal to mean that members of the Great Race are 'men' whatever that may be."*

"Why do you refer to your sort as the 'Great Race'?"

"Because of our superior intelligence."

"Superior to men?"

"We are men."

"Superior to the intelligence of earth men?"

"That is self-evident."

"Just as we are superior in intelligence to this poor creature Jerry?"

"That is not self-evident."

"Finished with the witness," announced Pomfrey. The opposition counsels should have left bad enough alone; instead they tried to get B'na Kreeth to define the difference in intelligence between humans and worker-anthropoids. Master B'na explained meticulously that cultural differences masked the intrinsic differences, if any, and that, in any case, both anthropoids and men made so little use of their respective potential intelligences that it was really too early to tell which race would turn out to be the superior race in the Third Planet.

He had just begun to discuss how a truly superior race could be bred by combining the best features of anthropoids and men when he was hastily asked to "stand down."

"May it please the Court," said Pomfrey, "we have not advanced the theory; we have merely disposed of respondent's contention that a particular shape and a particular degree of intelligence are necessary to manhood. I now ask that the petitioner be recalled to the stand that the court may determine whether he is, in truth, human."

"If the learned court please——" The battery of lawyers had been in a huddle ever since B'na Kreeth's travel tank ad been removed from the room; the chief counsel now spoke.

"The object of the petition appears to be to protect the life of this chattel. There is no need to draw out these proceedings; respondent stipulates that this chattel will be allowed to die a natural death in the hands of its present custodian and moves that the action be dismissed."

"What do you say to that?" the Court asked Pomfrey.

Pomfrey visibly gathered his toga about him. "We ask not for cold charity from this corporation, but for the justice of the court. We ask that Jerry's humanity be established as a matter of law. Not for him to vote, nor to hold property, nor to be relieved of special police regulations appropriate to his group—but we do ask that he be adjudged at least as human as that aquarium monstrosity just removed from this court room!"

The judge turned to Jerry. "Is that what you want, Jerry?"

Jerry looked uneasily at Pomfrey, then said, "Okay, Boss."

"Come up to the chair."

"One moment—" The opposition chief counsel seemed hurried. "I ask the Court to consider that a ruling in this matter may affect a long established commercial practice necessary to the economic life of—"

"Objection!" Pomfrey was on his feet, bristling. "Never have I heard a more outrageous attempt to prejudice a decision. My esteemed colleague might as well ask the Court to decide a murder case from political considerations. I protest—"

"Never mind," said the court. "The suggestion will be ignored. Proceed with your witness."

Pomfrey bowed. "We are exploring the meaning of this strange thing called 'manhood.' We have seen that it is not a matter of shape, nor race, nor planet of birth, nor of acuteness of mind. Truly, it cannot be defined, yet it may be experienced. It can reach from heart to heart, from spirit to spirit." He turned to Jerry. "Jerry—will you sing your new song for the judge?"

"Sure mike." Jerry looked uneasily up at the whirri
cameras, the mikes, and the ikes, then cleared his throat

"Way down upon de Suwannee Ribber
Far, far away;
Dere's where my heart is turning ebber—"

The applause scared him out of his wits; the banging
the gavel frightened him still more—but it mattered not;
issue was no longer in doubt. Jerry was a man.

THE END

NEL BESTSELLERS

NEL P.O. BOX 11, FALMOUTH TR10 9EN, CORNWALL.

For U.K.: Customers should include to cover postage, 22p for the first book plus 10
per copy for each additional book ordered up to a maximum charge of 82p.

For B.F.P.O. and Eire: Customers should include to cover postage, 22p for the first
book plus 10p per copy for the next 6 and thereafter 4p per book.

For Overseas: Customers should include to cover postage, 30p for the first book plus
10p per copy for each additional book.

Name...

Address...

....

Title...